MISS HARDING'S *Hope*

Also by Rachel Knowles

Available from Sandsfoot Publishing:
A Perfect Match (The Merry Romances 1)
A Reason for Romance (*The Merry Romances* 2)
A Single Obsession (*The Merry Romances* 3) (Spring 2024)
Engaging Miss Shaw

Available from Pen & Sword History
What Regency Women Did For Us

MISS HARDING'S *Hope*

Women of Weymouth

RACHEL KNOWLES

SANDSFOOT

Sandsfoot Publishing

This novel is a work of fiction. Whilst some of the names, characters and events portrayed in it are based on real historical characters and events, they are the work of the author's imagination. All other characters and events are fictitious and any resemblance to actual persons, living or dead, is entirely coincidental.

ISBN (eBook): 978-1-910883-07-5

ISBN (Print): 978-1-910883-08-2

Cover design by Miblart

Published by Sandsfoot Publishing, an imprint of Writecombination Ltd, 28, Sunnyside Road, Weymouth, Dorset. DT4 9BL

To my Lord and Saviour,
Jesus Christ
the Light of the World
and
the Bringer of Christmas Hope

For unto you is born this day in the city of David
a Saviour, which is Christ the Lord.
Luke 2:11

Chapter I

Dorset, England
June 1810

Peter Crowley glanced across at the pretty young lady seated opposite him, who was again attempting to draw him into conversation. She'd been trying to flirt with him since the mail coach left Salisbury. He met her latest sally with a bland smile and returned his gaze to the view.

The gentleman beside her—presumably her father or guardian—grunted his disapproval at the brief exchange. The man need not have worried. Peter would not have flirted with a girl little older than his daughter, even if she had caught his fancy.

But that was just it. She hadn't.

It was what he'd come to expect. No woman had stirred the slightest flicker of interest in him since the death of his wife five years earlier.

The thought aroused a familiar ache. Not the acute pain it had once been, but an emptiness that wouldn't go away. A warm memory, accompanied by a deep yearning for the love he'd lost.

He'd given up hope he would ever feel that way again, and he'd learned to be content. He thanked God he'd known the joy of mutual love once, and that would have to be enough.

Peter peered out the window as the coach stopped to change horses in Blandford. One stage closer to Weymouth and the only woman in his life now—his daughter, Annie.

She'd given his life purpose in those dark days after Beth had died. Someone to plan for. And he longed to be with her again.

The flirtatious young lady cast him a final wistful glance before rising from her seat and exiting the carriage. The harassed looking gentleman followed in her wake.

Peter chuckled to himself. Poor fellow. He had his work cut out, keeping his charge's behaviour in check.

The only other occupant of the coach—a middle-aged merchant who had fallen asleep as soon as they'd left Salisbury—didn't stir.

An elderly lady mounted the steps. Peter leaned forward to offer his help, but she just stood there, tottering on the threshold, staring at his outstretched hand, and then up into his eyes, a confused expression on her wrinkled face.

An urgent plea from a female coming up behind her seemed to bring her to her senses. Propelled into action, the old lady grasped his fingers, and almost fell into the seat opposite the sleeping merchant, but not before snapping a sharp reprimand over her shoulder.

Peter turned to offer his aid to the unfortunate recipient of the old lady's harsh rebuke—a much younger, red-haired woman, who struggled up behind her, carrying an enormous, covered basket.

To judge from the plainness of her garb and how she'd just been treated, he supposed she must be a paid companion, and his ready sympathy was stirred.

With a grateful smile, she relinquished her burden into his arms, and no sooner had she stepped into the carriage, then the steps were folded up and the door slammed shut behind her.

Before she could sit, the coach pulled away, and she stumbled into him, ramming the hamper into his ribs so hard that he fell back into his seat.

He gasped at the sudden impact, but wished he'd restrained his reaction when he saw the woman's troubled expression.

She bit her lip and shot him an apologetic glance. "I'm sorry, sir. I couldn't help myself. What a poor repayment for your kindness. Are you hurt?"

He was about to reassure her he was uninjured when he noticed that, rather than being filled with remorse, her green eyes twinkled up at him.

Something in their depths elicited a teasing response, accompanied by his customary, good-humoured grin.

"Not fatally."

Her face relaxed, and she glowed up at him as she took her seat. "That's a relief. I wouldn't know how to dispose of a dead body."

His nose twitched in appreciation. It was rare that anyone understood his sense of humour, and rarer still for someone to respond in the same vein.

"I believe you have something of mine," she said, smoothing out her skirts and patting her lap. "If you please."

Peter frowned at the cumbersome basket clasped in his arms. Her journey would be uncomfortable with this resting on her knees, and he felt the sudden urge to spare her.

"Is it safe to return such a dangerous weapon to you? I think I should keep it, or you might be tempted to attack again."

She glanced sideways, noting her elderly companion's blank expression before answering. "Alas, you've exposed my cunning plan, but without the element of surprise, I fear its use as an instrument of torture is over."

"But perhaps it might inflict a similar injury on yourself. I think it would be wise to leave it in my custody."

"That's most generous of you, sir, but I couldn't possibly let you keep such a treasure."

"A treasure, now, is it? I didn't realise a basket could be so versatile."

Leaning toward him, she spoke in a low voice, as if sharing a great secret. "It's the contents that are so valuable. Men would kill for what's inside."

With these words, she lunged for the hamper, but he refused to give it up. "All the more reason to keep it—to protect you from desperate men."

His actions made her pout, but the twinkle in her eyes was even more pronounced as she accepted defeat and leaned back against the squabs.

Peter wasn't sure what drove him, but he was conscious of an overwhelming desire to peep inside the basket, not so much to discover the contents, but to see how she reacted to his uncharacteristic daring.

Confident she was watching him, he lifted one corner of the cover.

A heavenly aroma hit his nostrils. Fresh bread and beef and goodness knew what else.

He was about to venture another teasing remark when his gaze flitted to the old lady, and he saw to his dismay that her expression had changed.

No longer staring into the air, her hawk-like eyes were fixed on her companion, and to judge by the look on her face, she was not best pleased.

The younger woman appeared to have noted the alteration in her as well. "If you please," she said in a resigned voice, patting her knees a second time.

Reluctantly, he yanked the hamper's cover back down and leaned forward to place the awkwardly sized basket in her lap.

"Thank you for your kindness."

He bowed his head toward her. "My pleasure. Peter Crowley, at your service, madam."

"Meg Har—"

"What are you doing?" the old lady said, cutting off her companion's words as she addressed him in the sharpest of tones. "Introducing yourself to Margaret? Such things were not done in my day."

"I apologise. I thought—"

"Ha! But you didn't think, did you?"

"No, madam." At least, not the right thought. It seemed he was mistaken to assume the woman was a paid companion. Margaret—no, Meg, she called herself—must be a poor relative, dependent on a richer one's will. It did not lessen his sympathy one jot.

"Humph! Young men today."

Peter was relieved her wrath had fallen on him, not Meg, and expected her to say more, but the old lady relapsed into silence. It seemed his deferential attitude had soothed her, for a while at least.

His gaze darted back to the younger woman, whose eyes danced as she pressed her lips together as though she were, with some difficulty, stopping herself from laughing.

Her dancing eyes drew a response from somewhere deep within him as the hidden connection between them grew. Hardly conscious of what he was doing, Peter's brows shot up, and he wiggled his nose at her until, at length, she gave in, and covered her mouth, changing the burst of laughter he had elicited into a cough.

The noise was unfortunate, as it drew the older lady's attention once more.

She narrowed her gaze and scowled. "I can see what you're doing, Mr Crowley, trying to turn my niece's head. It will take more than a show of kindness and a handsome face to win my approval."

She pinched her piercing eyes closer together as she inspected his person. "I suppose a man with your looks is *free* to pay court to

Margaret? I would have thought you would have been snapped up by now—unless you are not the gentleman you appear to be. Well, young man? Is there a woman in your life?"

Young man? He hadn't considered himself as such for some years, but he reasoned that a man of thirty-seven might seem but a youth when you were as old as the lady who was raking him down.

The ends of Peter's lips curled upward as his eyes darted back to Meg, who shot him a helpless smirk.

He twitched his nose, showing by the briefest of movements he had received and appreciated her sympathy, but it was quite unnecessary. He had far too even a temperament to be ruffled by an old woman's impertinence and was in more danger of chuckling than taking umbrage.

The temptation to be obtuse was overwhelming. "Indeed, there is, madam."

"Well, I never! What a brazen response. Pray desist from talking to my niece at once."

His glance shifted back to Meg, inviting her to join in the joke, but her eyes had clouded over with an emotion Peter had no difficulty in recognising. Sadness.

His pulse raced as he felt the need to wipe away that look. "You mistake me, madam. I was referring to my darling daughter, Annie."

Out of the corner of his eye, he saw the sparkle return to Meg's gaze, and something within him warmed in response.

"Hmm. I suppose a widower is acceptable. When did your wife die?"

"Five years ago."

"I'm sorry for your loss," Meg said, her expression so full of sympathy that it felt more like a physical touch. As if she had reached out and squeezed his hand.

Peter was unprepared for the intense reaction her simple words provoked, and he had to blink away the sudden moisture in his eyes.

The old woman scowled at Meg for interrupting her and locked her piercing gaze back on him, oblivious to the current of emotion passing between him and her niece.

"Then it's high time you took another wife. Where is your daughter now?"

"At a school in Weymouth."

"At school! You won't get her married by sending her to be educated, Mr Crowley."

Peter raised his eyebrows. "She's only fifteen, madam. A little young to be thinking of marriage."

"As I thought. Your daughter needs a mother."

"I thank you for your concern, but I don't wish to marry simply to provide Annie with a mother."

Her upper lip curled in contempt. "You're just like my brother. Refused to take another wife, and look where it got him. One daughter and no heir. Do you have a son?"

"I have not."

"Then you must remarry, Mr Crowley. A man needs sons. Daughters are a burden, not a blessing. They need husbands. Isn't that right, Margaret?"

Meg said nothing, but the heightened colour in her cheeks suggested she found her relative's line of conversation embarrassing. She shot him an agonised look, and with a gentle shrug of her shoulders, she silently apologised that she was helpless to stem the tide.

While the old woman ranted about the uselessness of her brother, the troublesome nature of men, and the right way to educate girls, Peter and Meg held a silent conversation of their own.

Using facial expressions and minute bodily gestures, Peter expressed his opinion on what was being said, and to his continued delight, Meg responded in kind.

At last, the drone of the elderly woman's voice dried up mid-sentence, and all that could be heard was snoring, as her snuffling joined that of the sleeping merchant, who had not stirred throughout the entire tirade.

Peter heaved an exaggerated sigh, and Meg's shoulders trembled, as if she were chuckling in silence.

If ever a lady needed rescuing from a tyrant! Meg must have a bottomless well of patience to endure living with such a woman. Maybe it was her ready sense of humour that saw her through the day.

He opened his mouth to speak, but to his frustration, she shook her head and raised a finger to her lips.

Peter glared at the old lady. Even while she slept, she had a hold over her niece.

Whilst he had no wish to wake her, he wanted to continue his conversation with Meg using words, rather than sign language.

He yearned to know more about this stranger who had connected with him on a deeper level than he had experienced in a long time.

In silence, Peter gazed at Meg, absorbing every detail of her appearance, from the plain straw hat that sat askew on her riotous auburn curls to the intense pair of green eyes that stared back at him.

Not a conventional beauty, and not in the first blush of youth, but it mattered not a jot to him. She had warmed something deep inside him during their brief encounter.

He could feel a part of him waking up. A part that had lain dormant for the past five years.

A wide smile spread across his face.

Perhaps he had been too quick to despair of ever loving again.

Chapter 2

Meg felt her cheeks warm as Peter regarded her with an intensity she'd never experienced before. She tried in vain to slow her breathing, but her body would not cooperate. Her pulse raced along as the novelty of the situation went to her head—and possibly further.

It was simply too exhilarating to be indulging in a flirtation with a gentleman—and such a kind one at that. If only it was more than flirting.

She gave herself a shake. The instant connection she felt with Mr Crowley—Peter—was irrelevant. It would do her no good to read more into his kindness than just that—kindness.

It was only Miss Whittaker's insistence that she should travel in the coach with her that had brought Meg across his path. A man like Peter Crowley would not have noticed her in any other circumstances. They would likely never have met, and if they had, they would not have conversed.

She would have admired his handsome face from a distance, and never had a chance to gaze into his chocolate-brown eyes or notice the silver specks that peppered his mahogany-coloured hair.

But it was rare for such kindness to come her way, and it could do no harm to dream, could it? To pretend they were equals, and could be more to each other, when, in reality, once this journey was done, they would go their separate ways, and never meet again.

She glanced sideways at her elderly companion—the bane of her life, but the means of her survival. Those first few minutes after she drifted off were always tricky. The slightest noise, and she'd wake, and there was no telling whether she'd be as lucid as when she had fallen asleep.

Meg judged sufficient time had passed since the old lady's lids had closed that she had sunk into a deep sleep. It should be safe to talk now. And though she knew it would not lead to anything, she intended to make the most of this brief oasis in the monotony of her life.

Her gaze flicked back to the man seated opposite her.

"I'm sorry. Miss Whittaker doesn't go into company often and I think she has forgotten how to restrain her conversation. If"—her eyes twinkled mischievously—"she ever knew."

Peter's lips curled into an even fuller smile. Meg thought it was as well she was sitting, or she might have fallen. She was sure she was not the only woman whose legs had turned to jelly when the full force of Peter's grin was directed toward them.

"No apology required. There are far worse things she could say."

"There are?"

"My employer—though much younger than your aunt—suffers from a bilious complaint. He is inclined to share more details about his condition than I care to hear."

"Oh no. How dreadful. The next time Miss Whittaker moans about her rheumatism, I must remind myself how fortunate I am that her stomach is robust."

"Does she complain a lot?"

"Yes. She forgets she has rheumatism and is constantly surprised by the way her joints ache. It must be very confusing for her. At least I'm a familiar face, even if she becomes confused and can't remember who I am. She probably thought you were somebody else. From her past."

"How worrisome. She didn't take kindly to my introducing myself to you. She would probably be quite horrified if she discovered I was not a gentleman of means, but only a steward managing someone else's property. A charming estate, I grant you, but not my own."

Peter grimaced. "If she knew, she'd have me thrown out of the coach by the ear. *Not a fitting suitor for my niece's hand.*"

He said the last in a voice mimicking Miss Whittaker's so well that Meg giggled like a schoolgirl in response. "I'm not really her niece."

She felt so at her ease in Peter's company that the words spilled out before she could stop them. She bit down on her bottom lip, waiting to see his reaction, fearing her confession would put an abrupt end to their conversation.

"Is that why you call her Miss Whittaker and not Aunt Florentina?"

Relieved the illusion could last a little longer, Meg giggled again. "I confess, I don't even know what her Christian name is, and it would be inappropriate for me to use it if I did. No one has used it for a very long time—at least, not in my hearing—but I'm sure it isn't Florentina."

"Miss W, it will have to be, then."

Meg gasped. "Please don't let her hear you say that. I can't believe you would be so rag-mannered."

"I'm not. But surely between friends..."

She tried not to let his words ruffle her peace. He was just passing the time. It meant nothing.

"Have you visited Weymouth before?"

"Yes, twice. When a severe bout of aches coincides with Miss Whittaker remembering the doctor's recommendation for sea bathing. She's always more comfortable after a few dips in the briny waters, though she complains it is a waste of time."

"Miss W seems to complain a lot. How do you bear it?"

Meg shrugged. "I pity her. It must be hard when your body aches, your mind is confused, and everyone you love has gone. The loss of her niece in childbirth last year hit her particularly hard. Besides, she's given me a home, and for that, I can accept any amount of grumbling. We each have our own burdens to carry. How do you cope with being apart from your daughter?"

"With a deep belief that I'm doing what's best for her. I couldn't look after her whilst running Mr Elsworth's estate. This way, she's getting an education—probably better than the one my wife would have given her. Beth had visions of launching Annie into society, but I won't have my daughter forced into a marriage she doesn't want. With a decent amount of learning, she can always teach to earn her keep."

"How very forward-thinking of you—to provide for the possibility of your daughter *not* marrying. Not everyone thinks of such things."

"Is that what happened to y—"

Peter broke off as a loud grumble erupted from his stomach.

Meg was glad of the distraction. It was a question she was most unwilling to answer.

He pulled a face at her, a guilty look in his eyes, as he patted his belly and laughed.

It was a deep laugh that enveloped her like a fur coat in winter, banishing the chill caused by his line of questioning.

After checking that Miss Whittaker was still asleep, Meg lifted a corner of the cover of her basket and peered inside. A moment later, she withdrew her hand, clutching a pie wrapped in a muslin cloth, and held it out to Peter.

"Maybe this will help."

He shook his head. "How kind of you, but I couldn't possibly steal your luncheon."

"Believe me, you're not. I can assure you, Miss Whittaker and I will not starve. We always travel with enough food to feed an army. I shall be offended if you refuse. The pastry is filled with beef and potato and the most delicious gravy you've ever tasted. Go on. Try it. You won't regret it."

He reached across the coach to take the pie from her hand, and as he did so, their fingers met. A tingling sensation shot up Meg's arm, and her eyes darted up to meet his, which did not waver. Did he feel it too?

For a moment, neither of them moved, but then she came to her senses, and thrust the pastry offering into his hands. This was just a dream. Tomorrow, it would be no more than a pleasant memory.

Peter unwrapped the muslin cloth and gave an exaggerated sniff.

"If it tastes half as good as it smells, it's going to be as delicious as you promised." He raised the pie to his mouth and took an enormous bite.

He closed his eyes as he savoured each mouthful. His expression left Meg in no doubt how much he was enjoying it.

"That must be the best steak pie I've ever tasted. I hope you'll pass on my compliments to your chef."

Meg's nose twitched. "I'll be sure to let her know."

"A female cook? I wouldn't have guessed. Is she married? I'm half in love with her already."

For the briefest of moments, Meg was tempted to admit she'd prepared the pie herself, but she stopped her tongue just in time. Peter was joking, and nothing was more certain to disrupt this amusing banter than admitting how at home she was helping Susan in the kitchen.

"How dare you?"

Meg shuddered at the sound of Miss Whittaker's voice. The poor dear must be confused again.

"Whatever is the matter?" she asked.

The old lady pointed her finger at Mr Crowley. "He's talking of love. Has he been meeting you behind my back? Going to elope, are you? Well, you shan't get anything if you do. I'll make sure of it."

Meg shook her head at Peter, begging him not to intervene. He seemed to understand and kept his mouth shut.

"I won't run away," she said in a soothing voice. "I promise."

Miss Whittaker sniffed hard, but didn't take her gaze off Peter.

"You must do things properly, young man. You may walk along the promenade with Margaret after church on Sunday, and then I'll decide."

Peter flicked his eyes toward Meg and gave a wry smile before turning back to Miss Whittaker.

"I look forward to it, madam."

Meg wondered whether he meant it, or was just being polite.

She hoped he was sincere, but feared it wouldn't make any difference.

If they met again, he would discover the uncomfortable truth about who she was.

Chapter 3

Weymouth, Dorset
December 1810

The bright sunshine of June had passed into the dark days of December. It was two weeks before Christmas and, once again, Peter was travelling into Weymouth.

As the coach bumped along the final stretch of turnpike into the town, his thoughts flew back to the last time he'd journeyed this road.

The memory made him wistful.

This time, there had been no Meg to capture his attention and stir up hope in his heart—and God knew he could do with some hope right now. His spirits had not been this low since Beth died.

The glimmer of a possibility that maybe he could love again had vanished like a puff of smoke. After that memorable coach journey, Meg had disappeared.

Perhaps it was as well. If Miss Whittaker had frowned on him as a suitor for her relative then, he dared not think how she would view him now.

He turned his thoughts toward more immediate problems as he trudged the short distance from the Golden Lion to Devonshire

Buildings, to the home of Jethro Hunt. His old friend always welcomed him into his home when he visited his daughter, but how would he react when he learned this stay might be somewhat longer? He feared he would overtax even Jethro's goodwill.

"Good afternoon, sir," a footman said, opening the door to him. "Mr Hunt's expecting you and asked that you wait for him in the drawing room. He'll be with you shortly."

Peter chuckled to himself. Neither he nor the servant expected Jethro a moment before his normal hour. His friend was so wrapped up in his business he wouldn't rush home early to see him. He would arrive in time for dinner at five o'clock. As regular as clockwork.

Having arranged for his trunks to be fetched from the inn, he made his way to the drawing room to wait. He would have liked to visit his daughter, but he knew better than to turn up at Miss Seymour's School in all his travelling dirt.

Jethro would not care if he sat down to eat without changing his jacket, but Peter refused to lower his own standards just because his friend paid scant attention to such matters. He would see Annie tomorrow.

Two minutes before five, Jethro walked into the room. He extended an arm toward Peter and shook his hand. "Back again, Crowley? Can't keep away, can you? You would save yourself a fortune on coach travel if you didn't make the journey to Weymouth so often."

"You know why I come, Hunt. If you had a daughter, you'd understand."

"Huh! I've no time for a family."

"True enough. You're married to your business—and she's a very demanding wife."

Jethro dismissed his comment with a wave of his hand and led the way into dinner.

Once seated at the table, with food on their plates, he returned to the subject. "You make it sound as if my business is running my life."

Peter was surprised. He hadn't expected his words to bother his friend, but it appeared he was wrong. "Isn't it? You never stop working for long enough to enjoy yourself."

"I pause every Sunday."

"For a few hours to go to church before your work lures you back. When did you last spend an evening with friends, or take a walk by the sea?"

Peter refused to be put off by Jethro's scowl and pushed on. "What about Christmas? It's the perfect opportunity to show me that your business is not ruling your life. Why don't you invite Miss Seymour and the other teachers for a special dinner on Christmas Day? We could have roast beef and turkey and mince pies—"

"You know I don't entertain. I couldn't possibly ask my cook to cater for so many people."

"Hire some extra staff. It's not as if you can't afford it. Annie and I could find some greenery to decorate the house—"

Jethro shuddered. "That kind of disruption to my household would not be at all amusing."

"Then come with me to Annie's school for Christmas. You know Miss Seymour would be happy to include you."

"No. You and Annie enjoy your fun, and leave me in peace to sit by the fire with a book."

"As you wish," Peter said with a sigh.

Contrary to his normal habit, Jethro didn't retire to his study after dinner, but accompanied him to the drawing room. Perhaps his words had done some good. His friend seemed keen to show his business did not hold him in its grasp.

"How long is your visit to be this time?" he asked, sitting down on a high-backed chair.

Peter hesitated, unsure of how to answer.

"It's two weeks to Christmas, so I suppose you'll be staying at least three weeks. I've not known you to come so early before. How did you persuade Mr Elsworth to give you so much time off?"

Peter dropped his eyes to the floor. What should he tell Jethro?

"I may need to trespass on your hospitality a little longer than that."

"Oh?"

"I've decided to take employment nearer to Weymouth, so I can be close to Annie."

"A sound move," Jethro said with a few brisk nods. "Where's your new position?"

"Lord Barnes is seeking a steward."

Jethro's eyebrows flew up. "The baron? I'm not sure that's a wise idea."

Peter's heart sank. He depended on this role. He stared down at his food so his friend could not see how concerned his words made him. "Why not?"

"He's not the easiest of men to work for. His temper is... uncertain. I suggest you think twice before taking the position. If you don't believe me, ask our parish priest."

Peter screwed up his forehead in confusion. "Mr Vincent?"

"No, no. Not the rector. Sadly, he's on his deathbed. It's the curate you should ask if you want another assessment of Lord Barnes. He's the baron's son."

Peter's heart sank further. If Jethro believed the curate wouldn't speak well of his own father, then it would be foolish to pursue this appointment. But it wasn't as though he had any choice.

"It might be a little late for that advice."

Jethro pursed his lips. "You've already accepted the post?"

"He's agreed to see me. That's all."

"And your position with Mr Elsworth?" his friend said from between gritted teeth.

"Finished."

"What!" Jethro crashed his fist down on the table. "You've left a lucrative role with a well-respected man on a whim that you want to be closer to your daughter? I despair of you. How could you be so imprudent?"

Peter remained silent, repressing the urge to defend himself. Much as he wanted to be nearer Annie, he hadn't chosen this path.

"You'd better pray Lord Barnes is impressed with your character reference."

Peter went one step further than that.

He prayed his old employer would send a recommendation—and he was not certain he would.

Because if Mr Elsworth didn't keep his promise, Peter wouldn't be able to secure a position with Lord Barnes.

Or with anyone else.

Chapter 4

The following morning, Peter ate breakfast alone. Despite his protestations that his business did not rule him, Jethro had already left for the warehouse. His scribbled note explained he needed to prepare for a shipment due to arrive that day.

Peter despaired of his friend. He and Jethro were so different, it was surprising they'd remained close after leaving Mr Dowling's Commercial School, where they'd studied together. His own seeming recklessness had annoyed his friend, whilst Jethro's obsession with his work concerned Peter. He hoped Hunt's determination to make his business a success would not drive him to an early grave.

On his arrival at Annie's school, Peter was shown into the headmistress's drawing room.

"How very glad I am to see you again, Mr Crowley," Miss Seymour said, shaking his hand warmly before offering him a chair. "Your daughter will be so pleased to know you've arrived in town—and so soon. The last of the other pupils only left for their Christmas vacation yesterday, so she has barely had a chance to miss her companions."

Peter was fond of Miss Seymour. She'd become a trusted friend since he'd first left Annie in her care five years before. He was privileged to see the informal side of the woman, which other parents and guardians didn't witness, as he always visited Annie during the vacations, when the normal school regime was on hold.

He'd often reflected it was a shame he'd felt no desire to become more than friends with her, for he knew his daughter adored the teacher, and would have welcomed having her as a mother.

But that spark of something had been missing. If only the teacher had been more like Meg.

The thought took him off guard. Since when had he started comparing women to the stranger he'd met on the coach, instead of to his wife?

Miss Seymour pulled on the bell cord, and a few moments later a maid appeared, who scurried away to fetch his daughter.

She asked about his journey and then turned to the subject of Christmas Day. "I trust you and Annie plan on joining us this year, as usual. And Mr Hunt, too, if you can persuade him."

Peter grinned. "I fear that's beyond my powers, though I tried. Again. But he won't be persuaded. As for Annie and me—we'd love to."

"Excellent. I'm relying on you to decorate the schoolroom. Joe depends on you finding us a tree, and I wouldn't want to disappoint him. Now we've become accustomed to the concept, I believe it wouldn't feel like Christmas without one. It's become a tradition for us, here at the school."

It warmed Peter's heart to hear Miss Seymour so concerned for Joe. Though only a foundling, she treated the boy as kindly as if he were her son.

"I'll do my best not to fail you, and—"

"Papa!" Annie cried as she burst through the door and threw her arms around him.

"Annie," Miss Seymour said, in a quiet but firm voice.

Reminded of her manners, his daughter stepped away and dropped into a curtsey.

"Good morning, Miss Seymour, Papa."

She pressed her lips together and glanced at the headmistress to gain her nod of approval before flinging her arms around him again.

"Walk?" he asked, returning his daughter's embrace.

She nodded vigorously and ran off to find her bonnet and pelisse.

"I can't believe how confident she's become under your tutelage," Peter said. "Such a far cry from the mouse-like creature she became after my wife died."

He met Miss Seymour's eyes. "You've been a mother to her. I'm eternally grateful."

The woman glowed with pleasure. "I delight in helping a bud to unfurl, Mr Crowley. It is what makes my profession not only bearable, but enjoyable. I do my best with all my girls, to set them up for the future, but it's my hope that Annie will soon have a more permanent mother figure in her life again. Some of us never recover from the loss of our first love, but your case is not, I understand, hopeless."

She paused and raised her brow in question. "Is it too early to wish you joy?"

Peter stared blankly at her. Why did she think he was about to be married? His eyes shot to the ceiling and back again as he guessed what had happened. Annie.

"Far too early! I made the mistake of telling my daughter about an amusing conversation I had with a young woman I met on the mail coach last June. Annie is of a romantic disposition, and she has built this up into something akin to a grand passion, when, in fact, I never saw the lady again."

Miss Seymour bit down on her lip in a gesture that made her seem more vulnerable than normal. "Ah, I apologise. I've placed too much emphasis on the declarations of a schoolgirl. Annie has not yet learned the discretion which comes with age and has, I fear, been a little freer in sharing your secrets than you would wish."

He let out a despairing huff of laughter. "So it would seem."

A moment later, Annie rejoined them, dressed in a warm pelisse and bonnet.

With his daughter's arm tucked within his own, they walked toward the seafront, passing the statue of King George III as they joined the Esplanade. Peter was still reeling from Miss Seymour's words, and the line of thought they provoked.

Would he have been engaged to marry Meg if she hadn't gone out of his life as fast as she'd entered it?

No. Not with the way his life had gone over the last six months—which brought him back to reality with an unpleasant thud.

What was he going to do if Lord Barnes refused to employ him? He couldn't rely on Jethro forever. Would he ever get another position as a steward after what had happened?

He glanced down at his daughter to find her gaze locked on his face.

"You're not happy," she said.

What was he supposed to say to that? He wouldn't lie.

"I am much happier now I'm with you."

"That's all very well, but when you return to Salisbury, you won't have me to look after you anymore."

His daughter's assurance tickled his sense of humour. His world had turned topsy-turvy if Annie was taking care of him, instead of the other way around.

"I'm not going back."

She stopped walking and stared at him. "Truly?"

He nodded. "I want to be nearer to you."

"Hmm. Are you sure that's the only reason?"

Peter inwardly cringed. His daughter was far too astute for his liking. How had she deduced there was more to it than that?

"I can guess what it is. You're hoping to see that woman again, aren't you? The one you met on the coach."

Peter didn't know whether to be relieved Annie didn't suspect the truth, or frustrated that she refused to let his attraction to Meg drop.

Her tenacity had caused him enough embarrassment already today, and he regretted telling her about Miss Whittaker and her companion in the first burst of enthusiasm after getting off the coach.

When he still thought he had the chance to get to know Meg better. Before his disappointment, that she had gone.

But now, when he wanted to forget he'd ever met her, Annie refused to let him.

"Have you seen her?"

"No."

"But you wish to."

Unbidden, a mass of red curls above a pair of green eyes, sparkling with amusement, popped into his mind.

"Aha. You do still like her. Your eyes are glowing."

Peter didn't bother to deny it. "It matters not a jot whether I wish to see Meg again. I only met her once and I've not seen her since."

"You told me she needed rescuing. Do you think she still does?"

"That's something we'll never know."

"Is it? What if I revealed that someone took possession of Miss Whittaker's house last week?"

His daughter pursed her lips together in amusement. "Wouldn't you like to know who?"

Peter would. Very much. If the old lady had returned to Weymouth, did that mean Meg was here, too?

He managed a brief nod.

"According to Joe, the occupant is a lady—and she is not elderly."

She paused for effect, and Peter waited with growing impatience for her to finish.

"People say she is Miss Whittaker's niece."

Peter's mouth went dry. He seemed to have lost the ability to speak. His heart beat so hard he was sure Annie could hear it.

Meg was here—without Miss Whittaker?

As soon as he could engineer it, he must call on her to find out. Would she be as eager to renew their acquaintance as he was?

And then he remembered his own situation, and his spirits plummeted.

He was no longer Mr Elsworth's well-respected steward.

He had no house. No work. And uncertain prospects.

It would be unfair of him to pursue Meg, however much his heart urged him to.

He had nothing to offer her now.

Chapter 5

Meg walked into St Mary's Church with Susan, in good time for the morning service, and looked around the building.

Nothing had changed.

The altarpiece depicting the Last Supper was still high on the wall at the front. Before it, the pulpit, and to one side, the pew reserved for the royal family. Half-way down the aisle, in the box pews to the right, was where they always sat.

All was exactly the same as she remembered—and yet, for Meg, everything had changed.

Because Miss Whittaker had died and bequeathed her an unexpected legacy—her house on Weymouth seafront.

It felt so odd to be there without the demanding old lady. Bizarre though it was, Meg missed her. Losing Miss Whittaker's moaning—her constant companion for so many years—had left a strange void in her life.

At least Susan and John had accepted her offer of a home and come to live with her. Without them, the loneliness would have been overwhelming. All the other servants had taken what was left to them and gone, but the cook—and her friend's faithful swain, the gardener—hadn't deserted her.

Meg eyed the familiar pew from a distance, grateful Susan stood beside her in the aisle, rather than slipping away with John to join the servants. How strange. It belonged to her now, but she couldn't rid herself of the feeling she had no right to be there. That she was an impostor.

She hesitated, wondering if she dared to sit there without Miss Whittaker beside her. Who was she to take the old woman's place?

She took a step forward, but peered back over her shoulder when she realised her friend hadn't followed. Observing the panicked expression on the cook's face, Meg shot her a quizzical look.

With a tiny shake of her head, Susan confirmed what she'd feared. If she sat on Miss Whittaker's bench, she would do so alone.

Was she brave enough to do it?

Meg's gaze lingered on the closed door of the box pew, and her stomach churned as a myriad of emotions passed through her—none of them pleasant.

No. This was a challenge for another occasion. She'd sit with Susan today.

As she turned to retreat with her friend, Meg noticed a man with dark brown hair. A familiar breathlessness overcame her.

She scolded herself. No matter how many times she was disappointed, every time she saw a gentleman with mahogany-coloured hair, she couldn't help but hope it was Peter Crowley.

At that moment, the girl beside him claimed his attention and his head tilted to one side, so Meg had a full view of his face.

She swallowed a gasp, hardly able to breathe.

It was him.

Suddenly, Miss Whittaker's pew seemed much more inviting than a place with the servants. If she were just across the aisle from him, surely he would approach her. Perhaps they could pursue the friendship that had blossomed so fast on the coach journey.

Provided he had forgiven her for not keeping their engagement to walk along the Esplanade, all those months ago. She hoped he would understand once he realised it wasn't her fault.

Susan grabbed hold of her hand to hurry her away, but Meg pulled it from her grasp. The desire to be Peter's equal, to be a woman worthy of his notice, was too great. It was a chance she could not pass by.

Head held high, and pulse racing, she walked down the aisle and opened the door to Miss Whittaker's pew.

It was the strangest sensation, taking her seat alone. She kept glancing around her, expecting one of the churchwardens to tell her she was sitting in the wrong place, but they didn't.

Meg took several deep breaths, and after a few minutes, her breathing calmed. She had a right to sit here. The house was hers, and the pew with it.

But no matter what she told herself, she still felt like an impostor.

Annie tugged on his sleeve as the words of the final prayer book response echoed around the building.

Peter glanced down at his daughter, whose face was alight with excitement as she whispered, "She's here."

His pulse quickened as he glanced in the direction of Annie's nod to where a young lady sat alone on the other side of the aisle. An unmistakable mass of red curls peeked out from underneath a dark blue bonnet.

It was her.

Annie grasped his hand and tried to make him stand up. "Come on, Papa."

Peter stared at the front of the church, refusing to move. He must stay away from Meg. He could not deny the fierce desire he had to talk to her, to see if the attraction persisted, but his circumstances had changed, and so, by the look of it, had hers.

She no longer appeared to need rescuing. Which was just as well, because he was in no position to rescue her now.

"In good time, Annie."

"But she's leaving."

Peter still wouldn't hurry. Nor would he let his eyes dart across the aisle to see if his daughter was right. That he was losing the chance to speak to Meg—the chance he'd been hoping for since they'd last met.

All this while, Jethro had been on his knees, his head bent in prayer, but now he stood and urged Peter out of the box pew ahead of him. Unable to delay any longer, he rose to his feet, and Annie took his arm.

Despite his obstinacy in staying so long in his seat, he harboured a hope that Meg had waited longer. He knew it was contrary of him, but he paused at the door to the pew where she'd sat, and at last, let himself glance at the bench inside.

It was empty. His heart sank as he realised his delay had succeeded.

He had deprived himself of the meeting his mind cautioned him to avoid.

But now the opportunity had gone, he discovered his heart still yearned for it.

Chapter 6

Meg wanted to sink into the ground. She was surrounded by strangers, and the only person she knew was ignoring her.

She had fumbled with her prayer book, intending to stand when Peter walked past, but he hadn't come. Although she'd spotted the girl seated next to him glancing at her more than once, he had fixed his gaze elsewhere. Did he find the painting of the Last Supper so alluring he couldn't drag his eyes away from it?

What a fool she'd been, to think he would remember her, and cherish the same warmth toward her as he'd shown when they met in June.

It pained her to admit it, but the message was clear. Peter didn't want to renew the acquaintance.

As soon as she realised, Meg couldn't get out of the building fast enough.

But leaving a church crammed with far too many people for its size was not a simple task. She was swept along until she reached the door, where the curate stood on the threshold, shaking hands with his congregation.

She joined the queue, fiddling with her prayer book, waiting for her turn to exchange greetings with the clergyman. When she was nearly at the front of the line, a lady came up beside her and touched her arm with a smartly gloved hand.

"Good morning. Pray allow me to introduce myself. I'm Mrs Frampton. And you are?"

Meg gulped hard several times. The stranger was some years her junior and dressed in an amber pelisse, which even she could tell was in the height of fashion.

"M...M...Meg Harding." She dipped into a curtsey, and the other lady bowed in acknowledgement.

To her surprise, Mrs Frampton linked arms with her and drew her to one side.

"It's a delight to meet you, Miss Harding. May I call you Margaret? And you may call me Eugenia. I'm sure we'll be the best of friends. I understand Miss Whittaker was your aunt, and you've inherited everything she had. What good fortune for you."

"I fear you've been misled, Mrs Frampton. I'm not her niece, and you exaggerate my inheritance."

"The relationship is immaterial. You were her companion, and she left you her house, and if you don't want to admit to more, I fully understand. It must be overwhelming for you to be thrust into society in a strange town, but you need not be anxious. I am not quite nobody here in Weymouth. Let me introduce you to some of my friends."

Leading her by the arm, she dipped in and out of the crowd, introducing her to select persons whom she deemed worthy of the honour. Meg couldn't help but feel flattered by the notice. It was a balm to her spirits, which had been bruised by Peter's defection.

She determined to enjoy the moment. She may as well, as she was helpless to prevent it.

Where had this lady come from? And why had she befriended her, of all people, as if she were someone whose attention was worth courting? It was a mystery.

A wicked smile crept onto Meg's lips. Perhaps she should explain her origins. That would send Mrs Frampton running.

If Peter wanted nothing to do with her, what did it matter if the entire town knew she used to be Miss Whittaker's maid?

But no. That would be a poor way to repay Eugenia's kindness, and Meg didn't feel brave enough to face any more rejection today.

Once again, Mrs Frampton drew to a halt, and Meg found herself standing in front of the curate.

"Good day, Mr Barnes. I'm sorry to hear of Mr Vincent's passing. The rector will be sadly missed."

"He will," the man replied. "Not least by his family."

"Indeed, I must condole with dear Cassandra. How brave of her to attend service today, without the support of her stepsister or brother. Pray, forgive me for me for deserting you, Margaret, but I leave you in safe hands. Mr Barnes, this is Miss Harding, a relative of old Miss Whittaker's."

Eugenia disappeared into the crowd, leaving Meg with the curate. She bobbed a curtsey before shaking his outstretched hand.

"I don't believe we've met—or have we?" he said, giving her a warm smile. "I think you might have come here once or twice before with Miss Whittaker."

"You're right, Mr Barnes. I was her companion for many years. She was kind enough to leave me her house in her will, so here I am."

"Welcome to the parish, Miss Harding. I hope you'll be very happy living in Weymouth."

"Thank you. I hope so, too."

But just at the moment, Meg doubted it.

She had been holding onto a dream that Peter Crowley would be glad to see her again.

And it was painful to let it go.

·♥·♥·♥·♥·♥·

Peter stared at the empty pew. It was only when the opportunity to speak to Meg had passed that he realised how much he longed for it. All the reasons for avoiding her evaporated, and he felt bereft.

The atmosphere in the church seemed suddenly stuffy. Hardly aware of where he was going, he let his daughter rush him along the aisle toward the door, where the curate was greeting his parishioners as they left the building.

"Good morning, Mr Barnes," Annie said in a bright voice as she drew Peter to a halt. "What an excellent sermon. Did you not think so, Miss...?"

Too late, Peter spotted his daughter's manoeuvres. She was already in full flow before he realised Meg was standing beside him.

The curate's lips twitched as if he, too, saw through Annie's antics.

"Miss Harding, allow me to present one of the pupils at Miss Seymour's School—Miss Crowley—and her father."

Annie bobbed a curtsey. "Oh, you don't need to introduce them, Mr Barnes. They've known each other for an age. It's so lovely to meet you at last, Miss Harding. Papa has told me all about you, so I feel I know you already."

"Indeed. I'm delighted to make your acquaintance, Miss Crowley."

"Oh, I don't think such formalities are necessary," his daughter said, linking arms with them both and steering them through the door into the fresh air. "Not between friends. Please call me Annie. Miss Crowley sounds so grown up, and I'm still very much a child, in need of a mother."

She accompanied her words with a dazzling smile, making Peter cringe with embarrassment. She was going to be the death of him.

How could he keep away from Meg when Annie was so determined he shouldn't? Bother the girl. She was practically begging Miss Harding to marry him.

Peter grimaced and shot an apologetic glance at the red-haired woman who had monopolised his thoughts for the past six months.

He need not have worried. Meg's cheeks showed only the faintest blush, and she regarded him with a decided twinkle in her eyes.

"You've told your daughter *all* about me? Just what did you tell her that she's so eager to meet me, after all this time?"

"I'm afraid Annie has a vivid imagination. I divulged how much I enjoyed your company on the coach journey, and she hasn't let me forget it."

"Did you want to?" Meg asked in a low voice that only he could hear.

Peter blustered, not knowing how to respond. It was a very forward comment for a young lady to make. But then, what had been conventional about their encounters so far?

"Would you like to take a stroll along the Esplanade with us?" Annie asked. "You needn't worry about your maid. I can be your chaperon."

"I don't have..." Meg glanced behind her, to where another woman waited.

"Oh, please," his shameless offspring begged. "You owe it to my father, seeing as you missed the walk you'd promised him after you last met. Isn't that so, Papa?"

Peter hesitated. He probably shouldn't let Annie have her way, but he couldn't very well retract the invitation made on his behalf. It would be the height of rudeness to back off.

Besides, perhaps he was being unnecessarily cautious. If he secured a position with Lord Barnes, his difficulties would be short-lived, and he would hate to alienate Meg if he might have a chance with her.

It wasn't as if he was asking her to marry him. It was just one promenade along the seafront.

And if his situation didn't improve, at least they could be friends.

"She's right. You *do* owe me," Peter said, offering her his arm. "Shall we walk?"

With a final glance at her maid, Meg nodded, her eyes shining with a pleasure that mirrored his own. Arm-in-arm, they headed for the Esplanade, with Annie a little way ahead.

Peter gazed down at the woman walking at his side, his entire being aglow with a warmth that was not accounted for by the winter sun.

What a fool he was to think he'd ever be content just being friends with Meg.

Chapter 7

Meg might be walking along the Esplanade, but she did not feel as if her feet touched the ground.

Since the moment they met, Peter Crowley had epitomised the ideal gentleman in her mind. Drawn to him by his kindness and his sense of humour, she was not impervious to his looks. Though his dark hair was streaked with silver, it demonstrated to Meg that he was past the age of silliness, and the softness in his eyes when he looked at his daughter was nothing short of adorable.

"Miss Whittaker took ill the day after I met you and insisted we return home at once. She died before the week was out."

"I didn't realise. I'm sorry for your loss."

Meg wasn't sure how to respond. Did she mourn her overbearing mistress? She'd wept no tears at the old lady's passing, but she did miss her, if not in a positive way.

"Thank you," she said, feeling it was expected of her.

"And so you are here, in Weymouth, without your aunt."

A wave of uneasiness flooded over Meg. Peter still believed she was someone she wasn't. "I already told you, I'm not her niece."

"But you were her constant companion."

"Yes, I was. Miss Whittaker was not an easy woman to live with, and my virtue was that I stayed when others didn't. I was never more surprised when I discovered she'd left me her house in Weymouth."

"Why wouldn't she desire to provide for you—her loyal companion?"

Although Meg trusted him, she couldn't quite bring herself to explain. Not yet.

"Why, indeed, when I've put up with her for so many years."

She hastened to shift the focus onto Peter before he asked any more questions she didn't care to answer. Avoiding the truth was too uncomfortable.

"And you? How long are you staying? Until the New Year?"

"Forever," Annie said before her father had a chance to answer.

Meg started at the girl's words. She had not even realised Annie was listening to their conversation. "I thought the estate you managed was in Salisbury."

He licked his lips, as if he was nervous. "It was. I mean, it still is, but I'm no longer Mr Elsworth's steward."

"He's going to work for Lord Barnes," Annie said. "Miss Seymour says his lordship's house is not much more than an hour's walk away, so Papa can live in Weymouth with me, and I won't need to board at school anymore and—"

"Woah there!" Peter laid a hand on his daughter's shoulder, a strained look clouding his features.

"One step at a time. I haven't secured the position yet."

Annie's face crumpled. "Oh, yes. I'm sorry. I got carried away."

With an unladylike sniff, she veered off to the right, hurrying over the sand, past the bathing machines, until she reached the water's edge.

Meg bit her lip in concern. "Is she upset? Should we go after her?"

Peter shook his head. "Better to let her sulk alone. You wait and see. She'll recover soon enough. Watching the sea soothes her spirits."

"Perhaps it would calm the King's mind, too, if he returned to Weymouth," Meg mused.

"I'm not sure even the sea could help him now."

"It's a shame he doesn't visit any more. I would have loved to see him."

"Annie would say you hadn't missed much."

Meg gasped. "She saw the King?"

"We both did, several times, in the year she started at Miss Seymour's School."

Meg plied him with questions, listening in rapt attention as he related all he could remember.

"I hold the King and Queen in high regard," she said. "They were amongst the few who merited Miss Whittaker's unqualified approbation. She approved of their piety and their devotion to each other—as do I. Not so the Prince of Wales, who revolted her with his extravagance and his libertine ways. As for the way he treats his wife..."

Meg glanced up into his face, trying to gauge if her opinions offended him, but she need not have worried, as he hastened to assure her that his estimation of the royal family was akin to her own.

They were still talking when Annie ran up the beach to join them.

Peter pulled a face at Meg, as if to say, "I told you so."

As they resumed their walk along the Esplanade, a gust of wind nipped at Meg's face, sneaking down her neck and making her shiver.

"Are you cold?" Peter asked, his voice full of concern. "Perhaps it's time we walked you to your house."

His words elicited a warm smile from Meg. He was the only man she'd ever met who'd taken an interest in her welfare.

"A little, but I'm not ready to go inside just yet. I love watching the way the wind whips up the waves, making them all white and frothy, and though it feels colder, I don't think it will snow. "

A grin sprang to Annie's face, and she barked with laughter, rolling her eyes at Meg. "Have you ever seen it snow in Weymouth?"

"No, but—"

"I have. Twice. In five years. And never before February. Miss Seymour says it's because our town is by the sea. It makes the weather more temperate."

"That's a good thing, isn't it? If the snow was too deep, people wouldn't be able to get to church on Christmas Day."

"I hadn't thought of that, though we could all walk from where we live. But Papa, how dreadful it would be if it snowed over the ridge while you were at work and trapped you there. You must stay in Weymouth on Christmas Eve. I couldn't bear to spend Christmas without you."

A deep yearning welled up inside Meg. How wonderful it would be to have someone wanting her presence like that. Especially if that someone was Peter.

He draped his free arm around his daughter's shoulders. "I promise I won't miss Christmas. Besides, Miss Seymour is relying on us to decorate the schoolroom and provide a tree."

Meg's ears perked up. A tree? What did they need a tree for? Miss Whittaker had never had one. But that was no surprise. Apart from going to church, Christmas Day had been just the same as any other for her mistress.

Meg realised she had no notion how the gentry celebrated Christmas. Below stairs, they had hung up greenery in the servants' hall and had a sumptuous feast, followed by dancing and some raucous games, and a kiss or two under the mistletoe.

Panic raced through Meg's body as she thought of all she didn't know. Inheriting a house was all very well, but how was she supposed to behave? Miss Whittaker had taught her how to speak in a genteel manner, but there was so much the reclusive old lady hadn't shared.

If she were to maintain the image of a gentlewoman, she needed to learn—and learn fast. Was it even possible?

A pang of guilt assailed her as she thought about how she had abandoned Susan to go with Peter. She had a nasty suspicion she would receive a lecture when she got home about aspiring to a position above her station.

But Meg couldn't tamp down the yearning to be accepted, if that's what it took for Peter to keep noticing her.

She was loath to betray her ignorance, but if she needed a tree to fit in with the other Weymouth gentry at Christmas, she must find out more.

What type of tree was required, and what was she supposed to do with it? She was desperate to discover anything that might help her. "A tree?"

"It's a tradition we inherited from my wife's relatives. Her mother was German and came over to England with Queen Charlotte."

"Oh my."

Peter laughed. "Yes, she had inflated ideas of grandeur from her connection with the royal family, and I'm afraid we didn't get on. She never thought I was good enough for her daughter, and didn't approve of me. But it's her we have to thank for introducing us to the custom of having an evergreen tree in the house at Christmas. We set it in a tub, deck it with candles, and hang twists of paper full of sweetmeats from the branches."

Meg's eyes grew wide at the picture his words conjured up. "That sounds pretty. What else do you do?"

"We bring in greenery, to cover the mantelpiece and trail over the doorways—"

"And we eat lots of tasty food, like roast beef and mince pies and plum pudding," said Annie, interrupting her father, "and play games until midnight. You must come and join us."

Meg's pulse raced. Could she accept such an invitation? Whatever would Susan say? "I...um..."

"Take no notice of her, Miss Harding. I'm sure you have your own plans for Christmas." He gave his daughter a kind look that took the sting out of his words.

"Annie has got ahead of herself in her enthusiasm. When we have our own home again, you may issue an invitation to whoever you choose to share our Christmas, but not while we depend on others. It's not your place to invite guests to Miss Seymour's."

Meg bit back her disappointment and hurried to reassure Peter. "I quite understand. It must be hard not to have a place you can call your own."

"Very," said Annie. "It's not fair that we don't have a house. My friend's family holds a magnificent entertainment every year on Twelfth Night, and no doubt she'll tell me all the details when she comes back after the holidays. I wish we could hold a party. I'm sure ours would be even better."

Peter furrowed his brow. "If you spend your time trying to outdo others, you'll always be disappointed. Learn to be content with what you have."

"Hmm. If you were so satisfied with life, why did you want to change your employment?"

He stumbled over his words as he tried to answer his daughter. "Being content with the way things are doesn't mean everything has to stay the same. Last year, Miss Harding had to find fulfilment, being companion to a grumpy old lady, and now she has to learn to be at peace with all the responsibilities of running her own house."

"That's it!" Annie cried. "We haven't got a home, but you have. You must hold a Twelfth Night party and invite all your friends."

Meg's throat went dry. She longed to please Peter's daughter, but she'd never given an entertainment of any description in her entire life—and the thought terrified her.

"I don't think I'm quite ready for that. Maybe next year."

Her words had a dramatic effect. The girl's shoulders slumped, and she raised her face to Meg's with such large, sad eyes she resembled a half-starved puppy begging for food.

Wisdom told Meg it was all an act, to get her own way, but she couldn't prevent her heart from responding.

"Let me think about it. We'll see."

Annie grasped her hands and danced round in a circle.

"Papa and I can be first on your guest list. We'll have a wonderful time. You won't regret it."

Meg hoped she was right.

Chapter 8

It didn't take long for Meg's normal positivity to reassert itself. How hard could it be to hold a party? She was certain they could manage.

Dismissing any fears from her mind, she let herself enjoy every minute of the Crowleys' company before they left her at her front door.

Annie threw her arms around her, hugging her tight as she said goodbye. "We'll see you again soon. I promise."

Peter kept back, shifting from one foot to the other, as if he was uncomfortable with this show of emotion. Meg held her breath as he stepped forward, and for a moment she thought he was going to copy his daughter.

But no. Instead, he extended his hand toward her.

What was she thinking of? Of course, he wouldn't hug her. He was a gentleman, and she was… trying to behave like a lady.

Grasping his hand, she shook it warmly before entering the house.

She slipped through the front door as quietly as she could, hoping to escape to her bedroom, where she could dwell on the flutter that Peter stirred in her heart.

"What the blazes are you playing at?" yelled Susan, striding into the hall.

Meg dropped her gaze to the floor, then shifted it to the ceiling, then the furniture. Anywhere rather than meet the anger in Susan's eyes—anger she knew she deserved.

And this was before she had told her about the party.

"I thought we decided you wouldn't pretend to be something you're not," Susan said, struggling to gain control of her temper. "But no, you have to go out walking with a gentleman. You're setting yourself up for a broken heart, and I won't stand by and watch it. Not without making a push to stop you."

Meg raised her eyes to meet her friend's gaze, imploring her to understand. "But it was him. The man I met on the coach last June."

Susan leaned back heavily against the wall. "I see. Then we have a bigger problem than I thought. You were half in love with the fellow having spent a few hours in his company, and to judge by the daft look on your face, your feelings haven't lessened."

"Is it so wrong of me to enjoy talking to him?"

"But he's a gentleman. People of our station don't marry gentlemen. You know that as well as I do. They might take a maid as a mistress, but it never means wedding bells."

Meg turned away. She didn't want to listen, no matter how wise Susan's words were. "We're not paupers anymore. We've got a house and an income. Why shouldn't we move in different circles from what we're used to? You saw how Mrs Frampton swept me under her wing and introduced me to the local gentry. They're embracing me as one of their own."

Susan huffed, but Meg refused to be put off.

"This is our chance to step out of the position we were born into, and become something more, and what better way to prove it than by giving a party?"

"A party? Walking out with a gentleman has gone to your head."

"Yes, a party. On Twelfth Night. Do this well, and neither Peter nor anyone else will question our past."

"It's all about him, isn't it? No care as to what'll happen to us if we run out of money or bring down ridicule on our heads. All because a good-looking fellow was kind to you, and you choose to imagine it'll turn into something more. It won't. So forget it."

Susan stalked out of the hall and disappeared down the servants' stair.

That was a bad sign. It meant she was more than ordinarily upset.

A few years her senior, Susan had taken Meg under her wing when she joined Miss Whittaker's household as a girl. They'd been friends ever since, and though the older woman's pessimism sometimes irked her, Meg knew she meant well. Was she being foolish to indulge in a dream that Peter might come to care for her? To love her.

Meg bit her lip as she remembered his initial reluctance to approach her. It was his daughter who had engineered the meeting. Was he too kind-hearted to refuse to walk when Annie had been so insistent?

She followed Susan downstairs. Her friend had her back to her, but Meg could see she was cutting up potatoes with unusual ferocity.

"I'm sorry."

The softness of her voice barely sounded above the noise of chopping, but it was enough. Susan put down her knife and wiped her palms on her apron as she turned around.

She sniffed loudly and grasped Meg's hands in her own. "God knows I love you as if you were my own sister, but sometimes you drive me to distraction. You're not thinking straight because of this man. We might have a house and a bit of money, but it doesn't change who we are. What's the point of building up your hopes on a lie? If he knew the truth..."

Susan's words hung in the air.

"You don't think Peter would consider marrying someone like me if he realised I was a servant, not a genteel relation of Miss Whittaker's."

Susan nodded.

"I'd like to believe you were wrong."

"Then tell him. Soon. I'm more than happy for you to be right, but I think it's unlikely."

Meg yanked her hands free from Susan's grasp and paced up and down the kitchen. Should she reveal the truth to Peter and risk him turning away in disgust? Was it even necessary?

"The difference between us isn't so great. Mr Crowley's not a gentleman of leisure. He works for his living, same as I've always done."

"But he's a gentleman's son, and earns enough to pay for his daughter to go to school, which we never could have afforded on our wages, and would be hard pushed to now. Our income is not large, Meg. It won't stretch to many luxuries. We might not be servants anymore, but we still have work to do. Who do you imagine is going to keep this house clean?"

"Hmm. I see what you mean. Couldn't John—"

"Don't you dare even think such a thing, Margaret Harding. He's no more a servant than we are, and I won't let you bully him into doing your share. We're in this together. John will maintain the garden and help me with the heavy work—"

"Which I'm sure he does out of love."

Her words earned a glare from her friend, but Susan's heightened colour confirmed she'd hit a soft spot. "And we'll cook *and* keep the house clean."

Meg slumped down on the nearest chair. "Oh joy! I was better off as Miss Whittaker's maid. I didn't have to dust and mop then. Can't we afford a servant to do it?"

"We could, but then we wouldn't have any money for extras—like parties."

Meg jumped up, eyes shining with excitement. "Do you mean it?"

"I'm a fool to encourage you, but I daresay I might be as eager as you to ignore my past if I'd fallen in love with a man above my station. Between us, I'm sure we're capable of laying on a feast fit for the King himself, and I expect we can stretch to hiring a few extra hands for the evening, but the rest is up to you."

"Thank you."

Susan huffed, but gave her an affectionate hug. "I just hope you know what you're doing."

Meg hoped so, too.

Chapter 9

The following morning, Peter set off for Lord Barnes's estate on foot. The day was chilly, but dry, and a weak sun struggled to break through the clouds.

Jethro would have lent him his chaise if he'd asked, but Peter already felt weighed down by what he owed his friend, and had no wish to increase the debt.

The walk would take him over an hour, giving him plenty of time to think.

He thought of Meg, and how patient she had been with his daughter, overlooking her rudeness as if it were nothing. She had seemed as eager for the reunion as he had been—without the reservations that had held him back.

Peter couldn't be sorry Annie had swept him along in her matchmaking plans. It was no surprise he'd been too weak to resist. How could he object to being forced into the company of the only woman who had captured his interest since the death of his wife?

But his conversation with Meg had left him feeling uneasy.

The gulf between their positions had grown in the past six months, and he was uncertain whether he'd ever be able to bridge the gap.

She was no longer the downtrodden companion of an elderly relative, crying out to be rescued. She was an independent woman, with a house of her own, who didn't need to work for a living.

He, on the other hand, was forced to rely on his friend to keep a roof over his head, and had to find a new position if he was ever to set up his own home again. If he didn't impress Lord Barnes enough to take him on, he would remain reliant on Jethro's generosity until he found alternative employment.

After an hour's walking and thinking, he was relieved to reach the gates of the estate. He followed the carriageway up to the house, passing through a well-stocked deer park. He paused for a few moments on a stone bridge over the river that fed into the vast lake in front of the Tudor mansion, which looked impressive from this vantage point.

As he started down the last stretch of driveway, Peter heard a chaise approaching from behind and stood to one side to let it pass. To his surprise, it stopped just ahead of him.

The door opened and the curate's head popped out.

"Mr Crowley, isn't it? What brings you out this way?"

"I've an appointment to meet with Lord Barnes."

"Off to see my father? In that case, I'll walk with you."

Mr Barnes hopped down from the carriage, told the driver to proceed to the stables, and fell into step beside him.

"Forgive my curiosity, but what is the reason for the interview?"

"His lordship is seeking a new steward."

"Ah. Yes, he is. Again."

Peter furrowed his brow in concern. That didn't sound encouraging. "Did the last fellow not stay long?"

"I am afraid not. My father is not an easy man. Few find they can cope well with his temperament—me included."

"I'm sorry to hear that, but I trust I'll prove to be one of those few. It takes a lot to ruffle my calm."

In the past, Peter would have said he was unflappable, but his recent misfortunes had led him to believe otherwise. Even *his* peace could be shattered if events conspired against him.

"Then the role may suit you, and if that's the case, I wish my father might take a liking to you."

"I pray you're right, for I have no other options."

Mr Barnes frowned. "That is not a comfortable position to be in. I hope he'll employ you."

They parted in the hallway. "I'm off to visit my mother. No doubt I'll learn how you fare when I see his lordship later. Good day, Mr Crowley."

Peter turned to the footman hovering in the entrance and followed him to the baron's study. After announcing him, the servant withdrew, leaving him alone with the master of the house.

The man behind the desk did not rise, but observed him in silence.

This gave Peter ample time to come to the conclusion that Lord Barnes bore no resemblance to his son. The curate was well built with chestnut brown hair and unremarkable features, with the exception of an expressive pair of deep brown eyes. In contrast, the gentleman before him had an angular visage, with an aquiline nose, cold, grey eyes, and a thin smattering of fair hair on top of his head. The deep lines on his brow hinted that his frown was habitual.

After a few moments, his lordship gave a curt nod. "Take a seat, Mr Crowley."

He sifted through the papers on his desk until he found what he was looking for.

"You say you were in your last employment for a decade? That's an admirable length of time. Why did you choose to leave?"

Peter wriggled in his chair. "I wanted to be closer to my daughter, who is at school in Weymouth."

"And your wife?"

"She died five years ago."

"Hmm. As good a reason as any for a change. It's as well it wasn't money, or you'd be disappointed. I consider your previous wages were generous indeed."

Lord Barnes picked up another letter and laid it on top of the first.

Peter recognised the handwriting as that of his former employer, Mr Elsworth. He gritted his teeth as he sat in silence, watching, wondering whether he was going to be given the opportunity to prove himself.

The baron's nostrils flared as he read, as if the content was not quite to his liking.

What had Mr Elsworth said of him? Had he supplied the promised recommendation—or not?

"It's a very brief reference, considering how long you worked for the man. Did you part on good terms?"

Panic seized Peter's chest and squeezed it so hard he could hardly breathe. How was he supposed to answer that without breaking his word to his past employer?

Before he could form a suitable reply, Lord Barnes banged a fist on the table and let out a scornful bark of laughter.

"Ha! Elsworth," he said in derogatory tones. "Now I recall. I thought the name was familiar. I know something of the man, as he resides in the same town as my brother. Believed he was as shrewd as they came until he got entangled with a woman half his age. I begin to understand your need to move on."

The panic in Peter's chest didn't subside. It did not augur well for him that Lord Barnes knew Mr Elsworth, but from the way he spoke, it did not appear he counted him a friend.

"Not surprised you upped and left. Easy to lose respect for someone like that. Now, let's take a look at things together. I'm a shrewd judge of a man's ability and character, so I'll soon gauge whether I want you working for me."

As Lord Barnes showed him a map of the estate and talked through the various issues that had arisen since the last steward had left, Peter's breathing returned to normal.

His uneasiness didn't disappear, but his natural optimism reasserted itself.

He thanked God that Mr Elsworth had upheld his end of the bargain, supplying him with a reference, albeit brief.

It was a huge relief, because only a fool would believe the baron would consider taking him on without a recommendation.

His lordship was giving him the chance to show he was a capable steward, and Peter meant to succeed.

He must. He needed this position.

So much depended on it.

Because without the next quarter's wages, he would soon run out of money.

He wouldn't be able to pay Annie's school fees.

And he couldn't pursue a relationship with Meg.

Chapter 10

Meg was dusting the mantelpiece in the drawing room when she heard a loud knock echoing through the hall. Who could be calling on them? They had no friends in Weymouth, unless... Could it be Peter?

She rushed out of the room, untying the strings of her work apron as she went, and hurried down the servants' stair to the kitchen.

"Someone's at the door, John," she said, bestowing her sweetest smile on the man sat in one corner, sipping a mug of ale while Susan cooked. "Be a dear and pretend you're our footman and answer it for me, won't you?"

Never a man of many words, he gave a curt nod and mounted the stairs to the hallway.

Meg shot up the steps behind him and darted into the drawing room before he reached the door. There was a mirror on the wall between the windows, and she checked her appearance, resisting the temptation to peep at whoever stood on the front step.

Fortunately, she had only been cleaning for the past hour, and she'd barely disturbed the simple hairstyle she'd adopted that morning.

After brushing her palms down her dress, to ensure it was free of dirt, she perched on a chair, placed her hands in her lap—as she had learned to do from Miss Whittaker—and waited.

A few moments later, the door opened, and John entered the room alone.

"Who is it?" she asked.

He held out an elegant calling card.

Meg read the name. Mrs Frampton.

Though disappointed her visitor was not Peter, she could not help feeling buoyed up by the realisation that she was mistress now—not Miss Whittaker—and the fashionable lady she'd met at church had come to call.

"She wants to know if you're receiving visitors this morning."

Meg took a deep breath. She supposed she was. "Please, show her in."

She rose to greet her guest as Eugenia glided into the room.

"Unforgiveable of me to pounce on you like this and ask you to receive me when you've barely settled in. I considered just leaving my card, but then, I thought, as we got on so well yesterday, we were a little beyond the formalities."

Meg murmured something which she hoped sounded positive and begged her guest to take a seat before sitting back down on the edge of her own chair.

Mrs Frampton looked around the drawing room, and then turned to her, with her lips pressed together and her eyes full of sympathy. "My, my. What a lot of work you've got to do here."

Meg tensed. She did? In her opinion, it was the most presentable room in the house, and it had far more furniture than any other. She'd been relieved she had somewhere to show her visitor, which need not embarrass her. But it seemed she was wrong.

"I suppose it is only to be expected when you inherit from an elderly lady," Eugenia said. "You can't expect the older generation to keep up with fashion, but *we* have no such excuse. You must let me be your guide. I've been decorating Mr Frampton's house, room by room, since we wed. Our drawing room is the pinnacle of my achievement."

A brief knock heralded Susan's arrival with the tea tray. Meg shot her friend a grateful look. She hadn't even thought to ring for one.

"Would you like some refreshment?"

"How kind."

It had always been Meg's duty to make and serve the tea, but somehow it seemed a weightier task when serving Mrs Frampton rather than Miss

Whittaker. Her hand wobbled a little as she lifted the pot, but she managed to quell her nerves and poured without spilling a drop.

Meg watched Eugenia over the rim of her cup as they sipped their drinks. Her visitor didn't say a word.

Oh heavens. She was the lady of the house now. Was her guest expecting *her* to say something?

As the silence continued, she wriggled in her seat. Growing desperate, she said the first thing that flitted into her thoughts.

"How do you and your husband plan to spend Christmas?"

Mrs Frampton finished her tea and placed the cup back on its saucer.

"In the grandest way, as is fitting for a man in my husband's position. You are new to the area, and may not realise, but he is the wealthiest merchant in town. We are holding a magnificent house party, with a ball on Christmas Eve, and a feast for our guests on the day itself. Mrs Fisher is creating something special for me to wear."

Her visitor paused and shot her another of her sympathetic smiles. "No doubt you will want to commission some new gowns, now that you're out of mourning. You need not keep wearing black forever. I'm sure your aunt would not expect it of you."

"But she wasn't—" Meg began, trying to correct Eugenia's misapprehension that she was related to Miss Whittaker.

"Hmm. Not pink with your hair, but maybe green. Emerald-green would look very fine with your colouring. You must come with me to my modiste. She's the most sought-after milliner and dressmaker in town. Not the cheapest—but the best never is. Yes, we'll see what Mrs Fisher recommends for your ballgown."

This could not be allowed to continue. Susan had warned her there was not much money to spare after buying what they needed to survive.

"I'm not planning to buy a new ball dress."

Mrs Frampton pursed her lips. "Next, you'll be telling me you will not attend my party, because it's too soon after your aunt's death to be dancing. I simply won't have it. You have been living too retired a life, Margaret, and it is time for it to stop. I insist you come to my party on Christmas Eve, and for that, you must have a new dress. If all your dresses are as sombre and plain as what you're wearing, it is essential that you replenish your wardrobe if you don't want to be labelled a dowdy."

"But—"

"I won't hear another word. I will not let you sacrifice yourself on the altar of duty."

Eugenia shot her a coy look. "I'm sure there is at least one gentleman in Weymouth with whom you'd like to dance."

Meg was powerless to prevent the heat that spread across her cheeks unbidden as Peter's face popped into her mind.

"Aha. So there is someone. Think how disappointed he would be to miss the chance to partner you at my ball. And if you wish to set your cap at him, you'll need something more alluring than that"—she wrinkled her nose as she nodded toward her plain but serviceable dress—"to wear."

Meg's resolution wavered.

She was gratified that the modish Mrs Frampton had befriended her, and she had no desire to let her new acquaintance down. Besides, she had no notion how to conduct herself in society and needed her guest's help if she was going to be accepted as Peter's equal.

And she would be lying if she denied how much she longed to dance with him.

Of course, there was no guarantee he'd be invited to Eugenia's entertainment, but what about the Twelfth Night party she'd half-promised to Annie? She would need a dress to wear for that, and there was nothing in her wardrobe at all suitable for a ball.

Surely, they could afford to buy a few dresses.

She pictured Peter's admiration as he saw her clothed in an elegant new ballgown, and her heart leapt.

Meg needed this. She must have a dress so she could dance with Peter.

She would face Susan's wrath later.

Chapter II

Peter set out on his walk back to Weymouth full of optimism. Despite the brevity of Mr Elsworth's reference, Lord Barnes had offered him the position as his steward.

He hoped he'd be able to weather the vagaries of his lordship's temper, and that he would remain in his employ for many years to come.

A short while after leaving the baron's estate, Peter was overtaken by the curate's carriage, and he was offered a ride back to town, which he hastened to accept. He was grateful to Mr Barnes for saving his legs, and for speeding his return to Weymouth.

He would have the rest of the afternoon to spend with his daughter—and enough time to call on Miss Harding and share his good news.

Although he'd intended to visit Annie first, Peter found his feet striding along the Esplanade toward Miss Whittaker's old house.

Just thinking of Meg brought a half-smile to his lips.

His mind threw at him all the reasons he should stay away from her, but his heart longed to unburden itself. To tell her the truth about his circumstances.

Besides, he had an offer to extend. Miss Seymour had invited her to spend Christmas Day with them at the school. He and Annie could show her the candlelit tree she'd been so curious about.

Before he was fully aware of it, he arrived at Meg's front door. He paused for only a moment before raising the knocker.

A footman answered his summons.

Peter withdrew a card from the case in his pocket and handed it to the servant. "Is your mistress at home to visitors?"

The man didn't say a word, but tilted his head to one side, as if considering the question, and then opened the door wide for him to enter.

Peter blinked in surprise. What a strange way to behave.

The footman's odd behaviour continued. Rather than announcing his arrival, he ushered Peter into the drawing room, thrust his card into Meg's hands, and left.

She rose to her feet, her cheeks turning pink from embarrassment—or was it pleasure at seeing him?

He bowed as she dropped into a curtsey, an urgent plea in her eyes.

What was she trying to communicate?

"Pray, introduce me to your friend, Margaret," came a soft female voice from the sofa.

Peter realised he'd been so focused on the woman he'd come to visit that he hadn't grasped they weren't alone.

An elegant young lady stood to greet him as Meg performed the introductions.

The name—Mrs Frampton—meant nothing to him. Who was she? A calling acquaintance, or someone closer?

The woman offered her hand to Peter, forcing him to take it as he made his bow. As she rose from her curtsey, she gave him an appraising look, sending prickles all down his spine.

She turned to Meg. "I am delighted to see you have a friend in Weymouth who is most presentable. You must bring him to my party on Christmas Eve."

Mrs Frampton flicked her gaze back to him, laying a gloved hand on his arm. "Well, Mr Crowley. Will you come? We'll both promise to dance with you, if you will grace us with your presence."

It was a harmless gesture, but the flirtatious behaviour of the gentry had never sat well with him, and he felt the stranger's touch burning through his sleeve.

He cleared his throat, which had become somewhat dry. "Shall we sit?"

"Where are my manners?" Meg said with a forced laugh. "Yes, please, be seated."

Peter took a chair opposite her, as far away from her guest as possible. There was something about the lady that made him feel uneasy.

"You haven't given me your answer, Mr Crowley."

He fiddled with the cuffs of his coat. "I'm unacquainted with your husband. I would not wish to presume—"

"Oh, fie. It is my party, and I may invite who I like. Surely, you would not pass up the opportunity to dance with Miss Harding and me."

Peter hesitated. Instinct told him to stay away from this woman. He doubted they moved in the same circles, and if he found himself without work again, he'd be even further removed from her sphere.

But there was no need to dwell upon such unpleasant thoughts. There would be time enough to mourn if that happened.

For now, if Mrs Frampton was a friend of Meg's, he would try to get on with her.

Besides, the lure of dancing with Meg was too great.

"I look forward to receiving your card of invitation."

"Excellent. Where are you residing?"

"With Mr Hunt, in Devonshire Buildings."

She pursed her lips. "Ah, I see. Fraternising with the competition."

"I beg your pardon?"

"Mr Hunt is in the same line of business as my husband. They are both merchants. Rivals. Only one can be the most successful dealer in Weymouth—and that honour goes to Mr Frampton."

Another reason he should be wary of the woman. He could not afford to alienate Jethro by befriending his chief competitor's wife.

She continued to talk about her husband's business with as much pride as if she had established it through her own efforts.

Peter let her chatter, occasionally darting his eyes toward Meg, but she kept her gaze fixed on her female guest, so he couldn't even resort to the silent exchanges they'd shared on the coach the day they met.

Unwilling to extend Miss Seymour's invitation to spend Christmas at the school in front of Meg's sophisticated friend, Peter resolved to stay for a polite fifteen minutes, and then go.

Annie would scold him, but it couldn't be helped. He'd return tomorrow.

He smiled to himself. It wasn't such a hardship to have a reason to call on Meg again. And maybe next time, he would be blessed with finding her alone.

When Mrs Frampton paused for breath, he stood.

Meg rose too, and at last met his eyes. "How did your meeting with Lord Barnes go? Are you to be his steward?"

It was a direct question, and both ladies stared at him, waiting for an answer. "I start tomorrow, Miss Harding."

She beamed up at him, warming him from the inside out. "I'm so pleased for you."

Mrs Frampton also smiled, but the flirtatious glance that accompanied it sent a chill running through his body, eradicating the warmth.

"Excellent. If you're going to manage the baron's estates, you must be staying in the area. I look forward to the opportunity to get to know Miss Harding's friend better."

Peter bowed toward her to take his leave, trying not to cringe. He had no wish to improve his acquaintance with a married woman, who was clearly bent on flirting with him.

He would tolerate her for Meg's sake—but that was all.

Chapter 12

When Peter had left, Mrs Frampton pressed her lips together and shot Meg a knowing look.

"Don't argue with me, Margaret. If you want to set your cap at Mr Crowley, you simply must have a new wardrobe. Any delay could be disastrous. Who knows what beautiful young women he will meet whilst working for Lord Barnes?"

"You mistake matters. I have no wish to—"

"Oh, tush. You need not admit it if you do not care to, but don't you dare refuse a trip to the dressmaker's now. There's no time to waste. I must introduce you to Mrs Fisher today. She's bound to claim she can't take on any additional commissions for weeks, but a word from me will work wonders."

A short while later, dressed in a dark brown pelisse and bonnet, Meg joined Eugenia in the entrance hall. The simplicity of her clothes had not, until that moment, concerned her, but beside Mrs Frampton's elegance, she felt outmoded and dreary.

Mrs Fisher's millinery and dressmaking shop was on St Thomas Street, close to one of the circulating libraries that Weymouth seemed to have in abundance.

Meg had never been inside such an elegant establishment in her life. Miss Whittaker had rarely ventured out, and all her clothes had been sewn by a local dressmaker, who had visited the house. The same woman had also run up the meagre supply of dresses in sober hues that her mistress had thought befitting for her maid.

Smart enough so as not to disgrace her employer, but nothing that Meg called pretty.

As they entered the shop, a girl of about twelve years old stepped forward and bobbed a curtsey.

"Good morning, Mrs Frampton. How may we help you?"

"I have a new customer—my friend, Miss Harding. We require Mrs Fisher's personal assistance."

The girl opened her mouth to speak, but Eugenia held up her hand to stall her. "Please don't bother to tell me the proprietress is too busy to see me, Martha. I'm sure she would not wish to upset such a valuable patron as myself."

Clamping her jaws shut, she bobbed another curtsey, and disappeared through a door at the rear of the room, presumably to fetch the owner.

Meg was uncomfortable with Mrs Frampton's behaviour. As a servant herself for so many years, she didn't appreciate the way the woman had treated the youthful assistant. Her words seemed threatening.

If such tactics were required to persuade the dressmaker to see her, she would rather go elsewhere.

It would probably be cheaper, too.

She was about to say as much to her friend when the door reopened. A lady entered, wearing a modest gown, with a fichu tucked in the neckline, and a white cap of fine lace on her head.

Even Meg, with her untutored eye, could tell that the dress—though simple—was well cut, and the lilac hue suited the wearer's complexion.

"Good afternoon," the woman said in a mellow voice. It was a soothing sound and a pleasant contrast to Eugenia's high-pitched tone. "How may I be of service to you?"

Mrs Frampton glanced at Meg, tilting her head and raising her brows, as if to say, "I told you so."

"Miss Harding has lately come to live in Weymouth, having inherited her aunt's house. As you can see, she has led a retired life, and her clothes are"—she gave a discreet cough—"a little out of fashion. I have persuaded her to put off her mourning and embrace some colour. And knowing how expertly you have furnished my wardrobe since my marriage to Mr Frampton, I assured my friend of your help."

Mrs Fisher pursed her lips, and Meg sensed the woman fighting her annoyance at Eugenia's tactics. However, when she spoke, there was not a hint of the aggravation she'd noticed in her eyes.

It had only been fleeting, and perhaps if she had not sympathised with the dressmaker, she would not have looked for a sign that she suffered the chagrin that Meg felt on her behalf.

"I would be delighted to help, but with Christmas so close, my order book is full."

A scowl passed over Eugenia's face, swiftly replaced by an ingratiating smile. "I'm sure you could find time to produce something for my friend to wear. I can't have her miss my party on Christmas Eve because she has no ballgown."

"A sad state of affairs, indeed." The dressmaker raised her index finger to her lips and held it there. "I wonder..."

She disappeared through the back door of the shop again and returned with a sea-green evening dress in her arms.

"It's half-made—a commission from Miss Mitchell—but now her stepfather has died, I assume she won't require it for some time. I must check with my client, but let us work on the assumption I'm correct. The colour will, I believe, suit you very well, Miss Harding. Martha, help the lady try on the dress. Mind the pins. We wouldn't want you to be poked."

Meg bit back a grin as she read the covert message the woman had given to her assistant. It was almost as if Mrs Fisher suspected the girl might stab her customer with a pin on purpose.

She went behind the screen, and Martha helped her change into the green dress. Meg's heart seemed to thrum louder and louder as the girl slipped the silk over her head. She felt she was being encased in luxury.

Regardless of how she appeared, she already loved the gown. The smoothness of the rich material was heavenly.

As she came out from behind the screen, there was an eerie silence. Meg glanced at Eugenia and then at Mrs Fisher, uncertain how to gauge their reactions.

Then she noticed the glow in the dressmaker's eyes, and the slightest upturn to her lips.

"Look, Margaret," Mrs Frampton said, drawing her forward to face the mirror on the wall.

Meg's gaze widened as she took in the sight. Was that elegant female truly her? Mrs Fisher was right. The colour suited her. Why, she looked almost beautiful.

Her heart skipped a beat as she thought of Peter's reaction. Would he think she was attractive, if he saw her now?

Deep down, a niggle of guilt tugged at her. Since when had her appearance become so important? It was what you were on the inside that counted, not what the outer shell looked like.

But that didn't mean she had to wear rags, did it? No. She was merely appreciating how the hue of the material made her green eyes shine and her complexion somehow brighter, more appealing.

"She'll take this dress, but that will not be enough. All her clothes are shabby and crying out to be replaced," Eugenia said.

"First, I need to check with Miss Mitchell—"

"Of course, but I cannot conceive what use Julia has for a ballgown whilst she's in mourning. I confess I'm surprised at her extravagance. I wouldn't have thought..."

Mrs Fisher's pursed lips were back. She must find Mrs Frampton's gossip as distasteful as Meg did, but was not in a position to complain.

The dressmaker moved around her, adjusting pins, and taking measurements, which she relayed to Martha in the same calm tone she had used throughout.

The latent irritation in the woman's eyes remained. It did not harm Meg's opinion of her. She felt more at ease with Mrs Fisher than she did with Eugenia, despite the frostiness beneath the dressmaker's subservient manner.

"Margaret will require a second evening gown, a walking dress, two morning dresses, a spencer, and a pelisse—"

"I'm sure that's more than I need," said Meg, trying to curb Eugenia's enthusiasm. If she was not careful, her friend would commit her to a complete new wardrobe, and however tempting, it was bound to be expensive.

Her income might sound grand to her, but she had the uncomfortable feeling it would disappear fast if she indulged in the purchase of too many clothes.

"Trust me," Mrs Frampton replied. "You'll present a very shabby appearance with fewer, and you'll need loads more dresses in due course. And hats. Oh, this would suit her, don't you agree?"

She selected a bonnet of gold-coloured velvet, trimmed with ermine, and held it out to the dressmaker.

Mrs Fisher flared her nostrils in disapproval. "This one would be a better option, as I have enough material left to make a matching pelisse."

She picked up a delectable confection of purple velvet and black lace and placed it on Meg's head. "See how well it sits? This style is very becoming on you, Miss Harding."

Meg's eyes glowed as she saw how elegant she looked. "Oh, yes."

The words slipped out before she could stop them. She pictured herself parading along the Esplanade on Peter's arm, dressed in such finery—and it was just too tempting.

"I should be most obliged if you could supply me with a dress or two, if it's not too much trouble."

"I'll do my best, Miss Harding, but—"

"Nonsense, Mrs Fisher. You always fulfil my commissions, however unreasonable the amount of time I give you."

The dressmaker bowed her head toward her friend. "It's a pleasure to meet the expectations of such an honoured customer."

Meg's nose twitched at the woman's ingratiating tone. Didn't Eugenia hear the veiled contempt beneath her smooth words? To judge by her satisfied expression, apparently not.

How Peter would laugh when she told him. Such details would not have escaped his attention.

"You will have the dresses ready soon?"

"I'll do what I can, Mrs Frampton. I am a dressmaker, not a miracle worker. There are only so many hours in the day."

"Then you'll have to work into the night to ensure I'm not disappointed."

Mrs Fisher chuckled. "I fear that won't be possible. My working day can't be extended. As a newly married woman yourself, I'm sure you understand."

A warmth lit the back of her eyes. "I don't believe Mr Fisher would take kindly to being ignored."

Meg bit back a grin. In those few words, the woman had stood her ground—regardless of how important Eugenia was as a customer. A minor battle had been fought and the dressmaker had won.

And she had revealed more, not so much by what she said, but by the softness of her tone as she mentioned her husband. Meg didn't doubt that Mrs Fisher was deeply in love with him, and an ache pulled at her own heart.

What wouldn't she give for Peter to look at her with that same warmth in his eyes?

Eugenia forced a smile, but Meg could see the woman's quiet assurance annoyed her. Had she grown used to her husband's money buying anything she wanted? Did it gall her to think a mere dressmaker dared stand against her?

Mrs Fisher wrote down Meg's direction and put the purple hat in a box. "Would you like to take it with you, or shall I have it delivered to your address?"

"Send it round," Eugenia said, answering on her behalf. "We are yet to visit the shoemaker, and I don't want to be weighed down with bandboxes."

"Very good, madam. And will you settle for it now, Miss Harding?"

Meg took a sharp intake of breath. She had been so caught up in Eugenia's enthusiasm she had forgotten there was a cost involved.

Would she have enough coins in her reticule to cover her purchase? Somehow, she doubted it.

"How much is it?"

Mrs Fisher named a figure that set Meg's heart racing. If that was the price of a single hat, what would the total amount to? Susan had said there was little money to spare. Would there be sufficient to pay for her new wardrobe?

The image of Peter's eyes shining with admiration clouded her thoughts. She knew she should back off while she still could, but it was so hard. She wanted this so badly.

These clothes were an investment in her future. To show the man she loved she was his equal and would make him a suitable bride.

And if she won his heart and hand, her finances would become his responsibility, and she wouldn't have to bother her head about such things again.

Meg gave herself an inner shake. It was all very well dreaming of a rosy future, but the reality might turn out rather differently, especially if she ran herself to a standstill.

"I don't think—"

"Put it on account, Mrs Fisher," Eugenia said.

The woman nodded and took them to the door herself.

"It's a pleasure doing business with you, Miss Harding."

Meg questioned whether the dressmaker would feel the same way if she realised there might not be enough money to pay her bill.

Chapter 13

The following morning, Peter breakfasted early with Jethro before starting out for Lord Barnes's estate in Dorchester. He pulled his greatcoat around him, glad of its warmth in the chill air of dawn. He'd been walking for half an hour when the wintry sun reluctantly rose, but Peter noticed no difference in temperature, as it yielded little heat.

The mist hung so low he couldn't see much of the fields on either side, but his thoughts were pleasant. He chuckled to himself as he remembered how Annie had scolded him for failing to deliver Miss Seymour's invitation. It seemed she was as besotted with Meg as he was.

He had assured his daughter he would call on Miss Harding again when he returned from work.

To his surprise, the day went well. Lord Barnes might be of a testy temperament, but he had a keen mind, and responded positively to Peter's observations when he showed him the estate books.

"Hmm. I believe my property will be in safe hands with you holding the reins."

"Thank you for your confidence in my abilities, my lord. I'll try not to let you down."

"You'd better not. I don't take kindly to mistakes."

The baron's caustic tone brought a sour taste into Peter's mouth. How different from his previous employer. If only he hadn't been forced to leave.

"Can you ride?"

Peter nodded.

"Good. Go down to the stables and talk to my head groom. He'll find you a suitable mount. You'll need it to visit the far reaches of my land without taking hours. Besides, I can't have you wasting precious time treading the road between here and Weymouth on foot. You can stable the horse at the Crown and ride in every day. Tell them to put the bill on my account."

"Thank you."

His lordship stared at him as though he had just uttered a profanity. "Ha! There's no need to be grateful. I'm not doing you a personal favour. It's necessary for you to do your job properly. That's all."

Peter pressed his lips together, struggling to subdue his chuckle. Was the man always going to keep him in his place in such a graceless manner?

If only he didn't need this position, it would be funny. But he was desperate to keep it—and the desire to laugh melted away.

The stable manager provided him with what he described as a reliable mount. Peter assumed that meant a plodder, and he wasn't far wrong. The horse wouldn't win any races, but his solidity appealed to him, as he rode out of necessity, not for pleasure.

He arrived back in Weymouth as the last vestiges of daylight disappeared. He longed to get beyond the winter solstice, marking the end of the darkest part of the year, when the sun set at such an untimely hour.

After stabling his steed at the Crown as ordered, Peter strode to Meg's house. He hoped she did not dine early, or he would miss her again.

His knock was answered by the same non-communicative footman as before.

Peter was about to enquire for Meg, but the man pre-empted his request by opening the door wide so he could enter.

He followed the servant to the drawing room and found to his dismay that, despite the late hour, Mrs Frampton was there again.

He bowed. "Good afternoon, ladies."

"The very gentleman we need," the unwelcome visitor said, before he had even sat down.

He tilted his head to one side, lifting his eyebrows as he glanced at Meg.

"Mrs Frampton is telling me her plans for her party. She wants my opinion on the theme, but I confess I'm struggling to offer any sensible advice. Eugenia is far more experienced at giving evening entertainments than I am."

"What do you think, Mr Crowley? Should I cover my ballroom in hothouse flowers, or strips of blue silk, like the sea?"

Peter shrugged. "I am at a loss to understand why you would choose to do either. The party is to be held on Christmas Eve, isn't it?"

"That's right."

"Shouldn't the decorations reflect the festive season we are entering?"

She narrowed her eyes. "In what way?"

"In my family, we have decorated the house with greenery from the woods for generations—holly and ivy and—"

A titter erupted from Mrs Frampton's mouth. "How quaint. I admire your persistence in adhering to a tradition passed down in your family, but it's not quite what I had in mind for my party. It might do very well for country folks, but I take my lead from London.

"When I learn the Duchess of Wessex is decorating her house in foliage, then I will believe it's fashionable. Until that time, I'll keep to one of my original ideas. Swathes of blue silk, perhaps mixed with white. Most appropriate, as we live by the sea, and unlikely to be copied, as few could afford the expense."

She tittered again, but then a calculating look crept onto her face. "Now, if you, Mr Crowley, were to hold a party, we could decorate your house with greenery, and then we could compare the effect. Perhaps you could persuade me."

Her words were innocent enough. Why did they send shivers down Peter's spine?

"Alas, it's out of the question, as I have no home of my own."

Her face fell. "I had hoped we'd have another opportunity to partner each other. Mr Frampton is not keen, and I do so love to dance. Perhaps—"

She turned to Meg, who sat beside her on the sofa, and took both her hands. "You must hold a ball here. It will be second only to mine in grandeur. I can supply you with recipes to pass onto your cook, and inform you of the best place to order your invitation cards, and where to hire the most accomplished musicians. What fun, to help plan your first entertainment. When shall it be? I know. Don't tell me. As the New Year begins."

"I...I..."

Meg shot him a wistful glance. The party Annie had envisaged did not include the likes of Mrs Frampton, and to judge by the regret in her eyes, it was not what Meg wanted either.

It heartened him to think that maybe the two women were not such close friends as he had assumed.

"I'm afraid you're wasting your time, Mrs Frampton. My daughter has already tried to persuade Miss Harding to hold a party on Twelfth Night."

He didn't admit that he believed Annie had succeeded.

Mrs Frampton was not deterred. She stroked her chin as she considered what he'd said.

"Yes, that might work. What an excellent idea! The perfect evening for a party. That's settled then. No strange customs for Twelfth Night, I hope, Mr Crowley?"

"That would be telling."

"Ah, I see. You choose to be mysterious. Well, you may keep your secrets for now. I must be going. Mr Frampton will be waiting for me, and we should leave Margaret to her dinner."

Peter saw his time alone with Meg disappearing. He needed to think fast.

"Pardon me, Mrs Frampton, but don't let me delay your departure. I must beg a few moments more of Miss Harding's time as I need to deliver a message from my daughter. Annie dotes on her, so I'm hoping she'll honour me with a reply."

The woman's false smile was back, but she kept it in place until the door closed behind her, leaving them alone at last.

Peter took Mrs Frampton's seat on the sofa beside Meg. "I'm sorry. I thought I was helping."

"Did you?"

"Yes. I don't want you to be forced into holding a party—by her *or* my daughter. They are both forces to be reckoned with."

"And who is the more difficult to control—Annie or Mrs Frampton?"

"Hard to say! Annie is so determined—just like her mother."

"What was she like?"

As soon as the words left Meg's mouth, a wary expression descended over her face, as if she feared the question might offend him.

His eyes glazed over as he pictured his wife. "A grown-up version of Annie, in looks as well as character. Full of life, always talking, stubborn to the point of exasperation."

"It must have been hard to lose her."

"It was, but her trust in her Maker never wavered, even when she was dying. It was me who struggled to accept that a loving God could allow her to waste away before my eyes—"

His voice choked on the memory, and he broke off as Meg's hand shot out and squeezed his arm.

"I'm sorry."

It seemed so natural to share his weakest moment with her. "I was a wreck after Beth died, but Jethro Hunt was a pillar of strength and he helped me trust God again."

"I'm so glad he was there for you. We all need strong people in our lives to prop us up when we're weak. Susan was a real friend to me when I struggled to adjust to life at Miss Whittaker's."

He laid his free hand on top of hers and gave it a reciprocal squeeze.

As they shared a moment of companionable silence, Peter reflected on the woman at his side. His feelings for Meg were deepening at a pace he couldn't control. He felt all the wonder of falling in love again—a thing he'd never thought to do.

Meg turned her gaze to meet his, her eyes twinkling with mischief.

"I have a bone to pick with you."

Peter raised his eyebrows. "You do?"

"Yes. You seem very set against me giving a party. First, you try to dissuade Annie, and now you try to put off Mrs Frampton as well."

"I've already told you—I don't want you to be coerced against your will."

"Is that so? And you're sure it wasn't because you were trying to avoid having to dance with me again?" she said with a roguish smile.

"Why would I want to do that?"

His voice sounded husky with emotion even to his own ears.

Peter swallowed hard. Meg's mouth was only inches away from his. If he leaned toward her, their lips would meet.

Her green eyes seemed to beckon to him, drawing him in. As if she desired his kiss as much as he wanted to taste her lips.

The deep longing inside him almost overcame his better judgement, but just in time, he came to his senses.

He dropped his arm and jerked away.

He couldn't kiss her. Not now, when he was in no position to offer marriage.

Not when she didn't know the truth.

Chapter 14

Meg sat, numb with the shock of Peter's rejection. Why had he backed away? Didn't he like her?

And then she remembered. She wasn't a servant below stairs anymore, flirting with the footman. She was a lady—or trying to be one—and he was a gentleman.

Meg shook herself. What was she thinking of? A gently bred female would not have raised her face to his, ready to welcome his kiss. Had she disgusted him by her lack of maidenly modesty?

His presence disrupted her balance so much she lost all sense of reason. Should she even be alone with him? Probably not. She knew she ought to care, but she didn't. She wanted to be with him.

Peter made her feel alive, as nobody else did. She'd been aware of it since the day they'd met. How she hated the rules of propriety that prevented her from gushing out her feelings like some infatuated housemaid.

It was pointless to pretend she had changed because she'd inherited a house and ordered some modish dresses. Meg suspected that whatever she wore—however fine—she would always be a servant on the inside.

"I've an invitation for you," Peter said. The huskiness had disappeared, his voice returning to normal.

Meg's spirits bounced back in response. Perhaps she had not disgraced herself after all. Ignoring the hollowness left by his rejection, she determined not to let her disappointment show and responded in an equally light tone. "Oh?"

"I'm afraid there's no fancy card—just me, sent as messenger. You're cordially invited to spend Christmas Day at the school with Annie and me." He held up his palm toward her. "And before you object, the invitation is from Miss Seymour herself."

Meg twisted her hands in her lap. Much as she wanted to accept, she feared Annie had forced the lady to invite her. If Peter's daughter had not restrained from using her persuasive powers on her, who was little more than a stranger, she didn't suppose the girl would be above wheedling what she desired from someone she knew well—even if that person was the headmistress of the school she attended.

"That's most kind, but I cannot accept. I don't know Miss Seymour, and my presence would be an unwelcome intrusion."

"I perceive what it is," Peter said with a frown. "You've taken Mrs Frampton's words to heart and despise the simplicity of our celebrations. Your friend declared that greenery is unfashionable, and so you want nothing to do with us."

"Don't be ridiculous. I'd love to see the schoolroom adorned with holly and ivy and mistletoe, and to marvel at the candlelit tree you described."

"But?"

"They don't know me. They are your friends, not mine. I would feel awkward."

And that wasn't all. Meg had never experienced being a guest in her own right. Anywhere. Ever. Though she supposed she must get used to that, if she was to maintain this illusion that she was a lady.

"I understand. Truly, I do. I felt just as uneasy when Miss Seymour invited me to share Christmas Day with Annie at the school, the first year she was there. She realised how hard it would be for me to entertain my daughter at Mr Hunt's. Can you imagine what havoc a lively ten-year-old girl would have caused in his well-ordered bachelor household?

"I accepted Miss Seymour's invitation because I wanted to be with Annie. To spend the day with her was more important than how uncomfortable I felt."

"What about your friend, Mr Hunt? Didn't he feel deserted?"

Peter shook his head. "He encouraged me to go. We attended the service at church together, and then went our separate ways. I tried to persuade Jethro to join us, but he dismissed the idea out of hand as he planned to return to his desk after dinner. He can't put the business down. I fear that one day it will kill him, unless he can learn to rest."

"Poor Mr Hunt. What a terrible burden to bear."

"Ha! He takes it on himself. But you? You were with Miss Whittaker, day in, day out. How was that any different?"

Meg sighed. It had not been the existence she would have chosen for herself, but it had been her life for so many years she'd never questioned it.

"I had Christmas Day off."

"I'm glad to hear it. Did you spend the time with your family?"

She bit back a chuckle. Her parents had sent her into service as a girl and she hadn't seen them since.

Her family had been below stairs—Susan and John and the rest of the staff.

"Yes," she said. "I spent the day with them every year."

"What about this Christmas?"

It was a question she hadn't cared to consider. There would be no dancing and games in the servants' hall this year, as it was only the three of them left.

Would they celebrate the day together? Probably, but Susan and John didn't need her. She was inclined to think she'd be in the way. Left alone, perhaps John would have the courage to ask Susan to marry him. Or—which seemed more likely—her friend would force a proposal out of him.

Which left Meg... alone.

"No. Not anymore."

"Then come and spend Christmas with us. Our pleasures are simple, but we always have fun. And if you still require persuading, have pity on me, because if you refuse, I will never hear the end of it from Annie."

Meg needed no more convincing. She stopped listening to the voice of caution and followed her heart.

"Yes. I'll come."

Peter leaned toward her, and for the second time that afternoon, she thought he was going to kiss her.

Again, she was disappointed.

Instead, he whispered in her ear, "I'm so pleased."

Although he did not touch her, the words sounded like a caress.

Meg hoped Miss Seymour would include mistletoe in her decorations.

And that on Christmas Day, Peter would find the courage to kiss her.

Chapter 15

The next morning, Peter rode across to Lord Barnes's estate, paying little attention to the scenery. Not even the chill air could waken him from his reflections.

He had spent a restless night thinking of Meg, and how readily she had turned her face up to his, as though she would welcome his kiss. The recollection sent a warm rush through his otherwise cold body.

Peter asked himself, for the tenth time, why he had pulled away. It was not that he lacked the courage to embrace her. If that was all it took, he would have had her in his arms before you could say Jack Robinson.

He had restrained his natural instincts, and held back, because... Why?

When he thought of Meg, it was hard to remember.

He supposed it was because he believed she deserved better than him.

And he feared he would be labelled a fortune hunter if he asked her to marry him in his current circumstances. He had made no secret of the fact that he yearned for a home of his own—and she possessed a house.

Perhaps it was concern for his heart. Did Meg feel for him as he felt for her, or was she just amusing herself, as society ladies were inclined to do?

He dismissed the thought as quickly as it had come. Meg wasn't like that—though he wouldn't put it past her friend Mrs Frampton. She was the sort of woman who might enjoy flattering her vanity with a little flirtation.

To his surprise, when he arrived at the baron's house, Peter found the hallway full of packing cases.

"Does his lordship have guests?" he asked the butler.

"No, sir. Lord Barnes is spending Christmas with his brother. They're leaving this morning, just as soon as the coach is ready."

Peter stifled a frustrated sigh. This was the first he'd heard of it. Didn't his employer think it would be useful for his steward to know he was going away?

"I see. And how long will his lordship be from home?"

The butler shot him a sympathetic look, as though he understood his frustration. "At this time of year, he usually stays in Salisbury a week or ten days, sometimes more, depending on the weather, and if there is any hunting to be had."

Peter's breathing stumbled at the mention of Salisbury, where he'd lived for so long. He recollected that his lordship's brother resided in the same town as Mr Elsworth. That was how Lord Barnes knew him.

What if they met again, and the conversation strayed to his reasons for leaving? Discomforting possibilities sprang to his mind.

With a nod of thanks to the butler for filling him in with the details his employer should have told him himself, Peter strode toward Lord Barnes's study. It was his habit to wait upon his lordship every morning, and he saw no reason to vary his routine. Besides, he needed to know any immediate concerns that should be addressed whilst he was away.

"Can't you see I'm busy?" the baron snapped as Peter knocked and entered through the half-open door. "Oh. It's you."

"I understand you are leaving for Salisbury this morning."

"What of it?"

"Is there anything particular you wish me to deal with during your absence?"

Lord Barnes wrinkled his nose. "Hmm, let me see. Ensure all the rents are in—no exceptions. And keep an eye on the drainage in the top field. You needn't ride over here every day whilst I'm away. Make merry. Spend some time with that daughter of yours."

"Thank you, my lord." Peter hesitated. "With a view to celebrating the season, I wondered whether you could spare a small yew tree and some greenery from your woods."

His employer sneered. "Why in heaven's name would you want that?"

"Annie and I mean to decorate the schoolroom for Christmas. It's a tradition of ours."

He seemed to have hit a harmonious note with his lordship. The derision fell away, and he nodded. "Ah, well. Tradition is always worth honouring. Help yourself to one of the saplings and as much foliage as you like. It won't be missed."

He waved Peter's dismissal and bent his head over his desk.

"I wish you a blessed Christmastide, your lordship."

Without lifting his eyes, Lord Barnes gesticulated with his hand again.

Peter didn't linger. He left, secure in the knowledge of two things.

He could gather all he needed to take the forest into the schoolroom, and he would have more time than he had hoped for during the Christmas holidays to spend with Annie—and Meg.

On Christmas Eve, Peter set out early for Lord Barnes's estate as usual, but this time, he was not alone. The day before, he had completed the work requiring his prompt attention, and this was a journey of pure pleasure.

He drove a small cart, borrowed for the purpose, and was accompanied by his daughter and Miss Seymour's man. They made their way through the estate, stopping at the edge of the woodland.

Peter hopped down from the bench and turned to face Annie, who jumped down into his outstretched arms. He swung her around—something she'd enjoyed since she was a small child—making her whoop with joy.

"Now, let's find ourselves a tree."

He fetched the axe from the rear of the cart and entered the woods. His daughter scampered ahead of him with all the enthusiasm of a much younger girl. He had to remind himself she was almost full grown, and it wouldn't be so many years before someone sought her as his wife.

Provided that man was honourable and upright, Peter would have to let her go. He accepted that by the time he could afford to reestablish his own home, his daughter might not require it.

"What about this tree?" Annie asked, bursting in on his thoughts.

He looked at where she stood and laughed. The yew her hand rested on must have been seven feet tall, if not more.

"Too big! Half that size would suffice."

She pouted. "But why?"

"For a start, it wouldn't fit on the table."

"We could stand it in a tub on the floor."

"An interesting idea, but I think not."

"But why?"

"It would take an excessive number of candles to light, and if we lit that many, we might end up setting the schoolroom on fire."

"You win, Papa, as I shouldn't care to do that. It would ruin the day."

Running a little further into the woods, she stopped by a much smaller evergreen, which he judged to be about four feet high.

"How about this one?"

He agreed with her choice and bade her move away while he chopped it down. Once it was loaded onto the cart, they turned their thoughts to what else they required.

Annie collected some ivy, whilst he garnered branches of juniper and yew, and discovered a plentiful supply of holly. The only challenge was to find some which the birds had not denuded of its bright red berries, but they soon amassed enough, and when they laid their finds in the cart, it was almost full.

"Time to return to Weymouth and start decorating."

"No! Not yet." Before he could stop her, his daughter ran back into the woods. Peter had no choice but to follow.

"Annie, we must go. I don't want to make myself late. Remember, I'm attending Mrs Frampton's party tonight."

"You need not remind me you are invited, and I am not—but if you dance with Miss Harding, I'll forgive you."

"You know I'm going for no other purpose."

"And that is why we're not done yet," she said, a smug smile on her face. "We must have some of that."

Annie pointed up into the branches of a beech tree, where several balls of mistletoe had taken root. Its white berries beckoned to Peter, hinting at the kisses that could be stolen under its shade.

He couldn't deny the thought appealed to him, but he feared the temptation would be too great. If there was mistletoe, he wouldn't be able to resist kissing Meg.

"I doubt Miss Seymour would approve."

"Pshaw! How can you let such a little thing as that put you off? Besides, maybe I fancy being kissed under the—"

"That's enough, Annie. If you can't be trusted to behave, we're better off without it."

She tossed her head back, poking her nose into the air, and stormed off through the woods toward the cart.

Peter looked longingly up into the tree. Did he dare?

Not pausing to answer his own question, he shimmied up the trunk until he was level with the lowest spheres of mistletoe. Retrieving the knife from his pocket, he loosened the nearest ball, letting it fall to the ground beneath him.

He walked back to the others, bearing his prize, with a smile on his lips and a spring in his step.

There would be mistletoe.

And he fully intended to use it.

CHAPTER 16

As the day of Eugenia's party drew nearer, Meg's excitement grew, and on Christmas Eve itself, her stomach fluttered nonstop with delightful expectation.

Full of restless energy, she completed her chores in good time, rather glad of something to pass the hours. Her final task was to lug enough warm water up to her bedroom so she could enjoy the luxury of a bath, relaxing her limbs and washing away every trace of dust and dirt.

Soaking in the copper tub, she revelled in the thought of the evening ahead, daring to dream. Tonight, she would dance with Peter.

Her pleasurable anticipation over the past week had been marred only by the fear that her dress wouldn't arrive in time.

If it hadn't, she would have had no choice but to cry off and stay at home, leaving Mr Crowley to dance with all the other ladies. The disappointment would have been unbearable, but she couldn't have appeared in a fashionable ballroom in a plain black gown. It would have been foolish to spoil her chances with Peter for want of a little patience. Not to mention embarrassing Eugenia.

But she need not have worried. Mrs Fisher had not let her down. By the time of the winter solstice, Meg was the proud owner of two day dresses, a smart green spencer with military edging, and a full-length pelisse that matched her purple hat, besides the sea-green ballgown.

Her eyes glazed over as she thought of the evening ahead. She knew it was vain, but she dared to hope Peter would admire her dressed in all her finery.

She'd seen him every day since he'd invited her to spend Christmas with him. Sometimes before dinner, sometimes after, always armed with an excuse for the visit, though she hardly thought it necessary.

They talked with the ease of old friends, although they'd known each other for so short a time. It was bizarre how close you could grow to someone in a few days whilst others were still strangers after many years.

Their last encounter, however, had been far from satisfactory.

After the service at St Mary's the day before, he had introduced her to Miss Seymour, so she could thank her in person for inviting her to share their celebrations at the school.

When she had turned back to talk to Peter, she discovered Eugenia had invited herself to join their walk along the Esplanade, giving Meg no chance for private conversation with Mr Crowley.

Tonight would be different. He'd offered to take her up in his carriage. Or rather, Mr Hunt's chaise, which he was borrowing for the occasion.

And for a short while at least, they would be alone together.

Susan helped her dress for the party, but the forbidding expression on her face throughout the process threatened to dampen Meg's exuberance.

"What is it? Don't I look the part?"

"Huh! Never fear that. You give the impression of the lady you wish to be. What I want to know is how much all this finery is costing us. I warned you—"

Meg refused to permit her friend's gloomy mood to cast a damper on her own.

"Not tonight. Please. Why can't you understand? For once, I feel as if I'm somebody, rather than the nobody I've been all my life. It might not last, but let me enjoy it while it does. Allow me to dance with Peter, and dream of a happy ending, like in that fairytale, of the cinder girl who marries the prince. When Christmastide is over, I'll face reality, and listen to everything you've got to say."

"Humph. Very well. I suppose you deserve it after bearing the brunt of Miss Whittaker's tongue all these years. I never understood why you didn't leave like all the rest."

Meg stared at her friend, willing her to understand. "Because she was good to me, in her way."

"The best thing that woman ever did for you was die and give you this house."

"She did more for me than that. Miss Whittaker gave me a home and I wouldn't know how to read or write or speak in a genteel manner if it wasn't for her."

"Hmm. Let's hope she taught you well enough. I fear for you. How will you cope when your dreams come tumbling down, as they're bound to do? If God had intended you to be a lady, you'd have been born one. It's not wise to rise above your station. Are you sure you want to go to this ball?"

"Yes. I'm certain," Meg said without hesitation, laughing and shaking her head at her friend in despair. Why couldn't Susan be happy for her instead of predicting disaster?

It wasn't a crime to pursue her dreams—her hopes.

To be a lady. Courted by a gentleman. To love and be loved.

When Peter arrived to take her to the party, there was no mistaking the admiration in his eyes, and Meg glowed with pleasure as he helped her into the carriage and sat down beside her.

This was why she'd spent the money on this dress. To witness him gaze at her like that. As if she were his equal, and he was courting her.

"Forgive me for staring at you so ardently, but I promised Annie a full description of your appearance. She had a fit of the sulks when she realised she wouldn't get to see you dressed for Mrs Frampton's party, and it was all I could do to dissuade her from joining me in the chaise."

"And what will you say to her?" Meg asked, before she could stop herself.

"I'll tell her the truth—that you wore a dress that matched your eyes, making you resemble some mystical sea creature—a mermaid, perhaps."

"I'm not sure if that is a compliment, Mr Crowley."

Peter gazed into her eyes and whispered, "It is."

The heat rushed into Meg's cheeks. The sincerity in his voice made his words intimate. Like a caress.

Her breathing became a little ragged. What would he do next? Would he kiss her here, in the privacy of the carriage?

To her disappointment, the vehicle stopped, and she realised they had arrived at Mrs Frampton's house. Peter's nearness had pushed other thoughts out of her mind, and she had all but forgotten about the party.

A footman opened the chaise door, and Peter hopped down before turning to offer her his hand.

Meg took hold of it, taking extra care on the steps, because of her unaccustomed finery. She was so distracted by the feel of Peter's fingers curling around her own that it was a mercy she made it down without slipping. It was just as well the sensation was tempered by the gloves they both wore.

Once her feet were safely on the ground, he held onto her hand a moment longer than necessary before releasing it, offering her his arm instead.

Meg's heart was fit to burst as she walked through the front door with Peter at her side. Maybe her hope that he would court her for real was not as preposterous as Susan thought. Why shouldn't she simply put her past behind her?

If Eugenia and her set accepted her, couldn't he do the same? Why did it matter that she hadn't always been a lady of substance?

This was where she belonged now. With Peter. As his equal.

These assertions brought a confident smile to her lips. She lifted her chin a little, as she'd seen Miss Whittaker do when giving a set-down to a presumptuous caller, and entered the ballroom.

·♥·♥·♥·♥·♥·

Before her was a sea of strangers. Meg recognised one or two faces—the curate, and another person Eugenia had introduced her to at church—but the rest were unfamiliar.

Elegant ladies, glittering jewels around their necks, their poise proclaiming their assurance of their own worth.

The women were interspersed with gentlemen, splashes of black and white amidst the dazzling spread of colours of the ballgowns. All standing tall. All secure in the knowledge that they belonged.

Meg's boldness fled. Her stomach turned in somersaults as the hollowness of her previous assertions hit her.

She was deceiving herself. This was not her world.

Would she make a fool of herself? Say something that revealed her humble beginnings? Embarrass herself—or worse still, the man she loved?

Meg held onto Peter's arm as if it were a life-preserver, and tried not to feel like an imposter. Together they approached Eugenia, who stood just inside the room.

She welcomed them enthusiastically, before introducing the middle-aged gentleman beside her as her husband.

Meg's first impression of Mr Frampton was not favourable. His wife had to lay her hand on his arm in order to drag his attention away from the man on his other side for long enough to greet them.

The smile that accompanied his bow was genial, but his greeting was as curt as politeness allowed, and as soon as it was over, he returned to the conversation their arrival had interrupted.

Meg saw a frown flit across her friend's features, as if she disapproved of her spouse turning away from her guests so fast, and her ready compassion was aroused. In her opinion, Mr Frampton's wealth was poor compensation for being saddled with an unpleasant husband.

However, when Eugenia turned back to address her, there was no hint that she desired Meg's sympathy. Any sign of discontent had vanished.

"Mrs Fisher was right about the colour. You look radiant in that dress. Wouldn't you agree, Mr Crowley? I know you must, because I see you can't take your eyes off Miss Harding."

"Indeed, I do. She looks absolutely beautiful."

A fresh wave of heat warmed Meg's cheeks, brought on by her friend's embarrassing behaviour. Did Eugenia think Peter would only pay her a compliment if she forced it out of him, or was this just the way ladies talked in society?

And though it was pleasant to hear him call her beautiful, the words seemed flat compared to what he had said to her in the carriage.

"I must see to my other guests. Don't forget our dance, Mr Crowley."

He bowed his head in acknowledgement and moved further into the room. Meg clung to him, pulse racing as her nerves threatened to overwhelm her.

Why had she come? She didn't belong here with these people.

Without realising what she was doing, she tightened her grasp on his arm.

Peter glanced at her, a question in his eyes.

"Don't leave me. Please," she whispered.

He gave a wry smile and led her across the room to where a servant was serving drinks.

"Would you like some orgeat?"

Meg hesitated. Would she? She didn't know, as she'd never tasted it. She wasn't even sure what it was. What if it was so revolting she wanted to spit it out? Perhaps it would be better to refuse.

"I think not. It may curdle my insides."

Peter grinned. "I can't abide the stuff either. Lemonade it is."

She returned his smile and accepted his choice, hoping it would not taste as bitter as it sounded.

Having obtained two glasses of lemonade, he led the way to one side of the room where chairs lined the walls, and motioned for her to sit.

Meg contemplated the glass in her hands and gingerly took a sip. It was a relief to discover the drink was more palatable than she'd feared. Better than palatable—delicious. It must have lots of sugar in.

She glanced up to find Peter watching her.

"Why are you staring at me? Have I spilt some on my dress?"

He chuckled. It was a deep throaty chuckle which did funny things to her insides. "Why assume something is wrong? Maybe I like what I'm looking at."

Meg eyed him warily. Was he offering her Spanish coin, or did he mean what he said?

"Would you do me the honour of standing up with me for the next?"

His gaze did not waver as he waited for her answer, his expression that of a man confident he wouldn't be refused.

This was the moment she had longed for, and yet now it had arrived, Meg hesitated. She had no experience of participating in a ball. Would she step on her partner's feet and embarrass them both?

She glanced across at where the dancing was in progress and froze.

What was it? A cotillion? She wasn't sure, but its name was irrelevant. It wasn't one of the country dances with which she was familiar and she didn't know the steps.

Her throat went dry, and she gulped hard several times. She would have to cry off.

The smile faded from Peter's lips. "Are you unwell?"

"No, I am quite well, but I don't intend to dance."

Meg's heart hiccupped at the hurt in his eyes.

"I see. I thought..."

She could not let this go on. She had to tell him the truth. Explain why she felt unable to stand up with him, even though she'd come with that very object in view.

"I want to dance with you, Peter, truly I do, but this"—she waved her hand around the ballroom—"is not my world. I've never attended a ball like this in my life. My experience of dancing is limited to impromptu hops in the servants' hall. Inheriting Miss Whittaker's house has altered my position in society, but it hasn't changed who I am in here."

She patted her heart and looked at Peter, hoping, desperately, that he would not walk away from her now he knew of her humble origins.

He let out an exaggerated sigh. "And there was me thinking you were trying to avoid dancing with me."

"You're not angry?"

"Angry? No. I should have recalled what a restricted life you led as Miss Whittaker's companion while she was alive. Even the redoubtable Miss Harding is allowed to have qualms facing a society ballroom for the first time. It can be quite intimidating, and I confess I much prefer the sound of an informal hop to this, but don't tell your friend, Mrs Frampton, that I said so."

His eyes twinkled as he grabbed her hand, a wicked grin on his lips.

"What are you doing?"

"Leading you into the set."

"But I told you—"

"That you wished to dance with me. And as I desire to dance with you, we shall have to muddle through the steps as best we can. If they call a dance you don't know, wink at me, and we'll excuse ourselves until the next."

She couldn't resist Peter's entreaties, and let him steer her to the bottom of the set.

A niggle of guilt pricked her conscience. He hadn't grasped the full import of her words—that she had been a servant, and not merely a companion with a restricted social life.

Meg wanted to undeceive him, but she didn't have the heart to try again tonight.

Especially not when she recognised the next dance that was called.

Her body shook with silent laughter as Peter raised his eyebrows in question.

No wink was necessary.

Chapter 17

Peter knew he should keep his distance, but he seemed unable to act rationally where Meg was concerned. He wanted her in his arms—but given that was impossible, dancing was the next best thing.

He realised he was beyond the point of retreat when she had refused to dance with him. The way his heart plummeted confirmed what he already knew.

He was in love with Meg—and he couldn't tell her. Not while his future was so uncertain.

He was so wrapped up in his thoughts that he missed his step and almost trod on her foot.

"You didn't warn me I'd need iron slippers to dance with you."

Peter's nose twitched with amusement. He was glad of the reprieve from the serious bent his mind had taken and answered her in kind.

"I feared it would draw too much attention to your mistakes."

"*My* mistakes?"

"I assumed there would be many as you told me this was your first ball. Unless you're not telling me the truth..."

A blush suffused Meg's cheeks. He couldn't be sure whether it was because of the exertions of the dance, or if his words had unsettled her.

"Perhaps the dances are less different than you feared," he said, hastening to reassure her.

"Perhaps they are."

Peter was glad he had forced her to stand up with him. If she had continued to refuse, it would have sucked all the enjoyment out of dancing, and he would have been tempted not to join in himself.

To judge by her glowing face, Meg was enjoying it as much as he was, and he hoped she would feel confident to take part in the rest of the evening's entertainment.

If only he could partner her in every set.

"How many dresses do you calculate you could make out of Eugenia's decorations?"

Decorations? What decorations? His attention had been so fixed on Meg that he hadn't even noticed the swathes of blue and white fabric draped over the walls.

"A dozen, I reckon," she said. "What do you think?"

Peter furrowed his brow. What an unusual thing to consider. Was it mere idle speculation, or did she have some purpose in following this line of thought?

He observed the number of strips of cloth and the generous folds of the material, and performed some computations in his head before replying. "Twenty-five."

"That many?"

"I believe so, though we can't prove I'm right unless the silk is actually turned into dresses."

"Hmm. It would be marvellous if we could. I wonder what Eugenia intends to do with it."

"I doubt she's given it a moment's thought."

Her eyes lit up. "No, but if I put the idea in her mind, perhaps she will donate it to a charity school or an orphanage. The material is too fine for everyday use, but it would make lovely gowns for the poor girls to wear to church on Sunday."

Peter didn't think Mrs Frampton would share Meg's enthusiasm, but was happy to be proved wrong. It was a kind-hearted notion, and he was touched she would even consider such a thing, while dancing at a ball.

At the end of the set, he bowed to his partner, who dipped into a curtsey deep enough for a duke. He accepted the compliment, but wished it was nearer to the truth.

The curate claimed Meg's hand for the next, and Peter was left alone, propping up the rear wall of the ballroom, trying not to follow her with jealous eyes. As the son of the baron whom he worked for, Mr Barnes was a far better match than he.

To admit as much weighed on his heart, masking the pleasure of his dance with Meg, like a cloud blocking out the sun.

Peter knew he should stand up with one of the ladies without a partner casting hopeful glances in his direction, but he struggled to find the enthusiasm to ask any of them.

Some words floated into his mind. Words that Mr Barnes had spoken in church the day before. *Think of others before yourself.* Like Meg had just done.

He uttered a quick prayer of contrition and, spotting a lady with whom he had a slight acquaintance, he asked her to stand up with him. Her delight at the invitation was obvious, and it warmed Peter's heart, knowing he was doing his Christian duty.

Her clumsy steps only slightly tempered his enjoyment, as her lack of conversation gave him plenty of opportunity to scan the room for Meg.

He found her and Mr Barnes at the far end of the set, where she was dancing like an angel, despite her inexperience.

Peter was glad she seemed to be enjoying herself. But—though it was selfish of him—he hoped she was not enjoying herself too much.

After standing up for several more sets with slight acquaintances, he felt he had done his duty and left it long enough before asking Meg to dance again. He had timed it so she would be his supper partner, and having noticed where she was in the set, he hastened in her direction as soon as the music ended.

He cast a wistful glance at the decorations as he made his way toward her. If only Mrs Frampton had arrayed her ballroom in greenery rather than fabric, there might have been mistletoe.

As if the thought had conjured up the woman, she appeared in front of him.

"Come for our dance, Mr Crowley?"

Peter tamped down his frustration and bowed to his hostess. Politeness forced his hand. "Would you do me the honour of the next?"

Mrs Frampton gleamed. "I would indeed. I've been looking forward to it all evening."

He gritted his teeth, trying to brush off her words. Such talk was the way of society. She meant nothing by it—or did she?

Perhaps it was just as well there was no mistletoe in the room. He would have been on tenterhooks during the entire ball, ensuring that Mrs Frampton did not lure him under it.

He held out his arm and led her into the dance, passing close to Meg as he went. Regret tugged at him when he noticed the disappointment on her face—a disappointment that mirrored his own.

Peter hoped she would not be obliged to sit out the next because of the lack of a partner, but retracted the thought when Mr Barnes asked her to stand up with him a second time.

He told himself the curate was just being friendly to a newcomer to the town, but he couldn't stop himself from wishing they could swap partners.

And it made him twice as thankful there was no mistletoe. He could not have stomached witnessing Meg kiss anyone else under it.

When their dances ended, Peter led Mrs Frampton into the supper room. He could not escape her company, but he managed to obtain Meg's too, by securing them places opposite her and Mr Barnes.

The opulence of the ballroom was echoed at the supper table, which boasted a vast array of dishes. If Mrs Frampton wanted to impress her guests, she had succeeded. Meg's eyes grew wide as she observed the variety of food laid out, and Peter suspected she had never seen such a grand spread.

Once their plates were filled, Meg wasted no time bringing up the subject of the decorations.

"I was wondering what you planned to do with the fabric after the ball."

"Do?"

"I thought it could be used for the purpose for which it was intended—to make dresses."

Mrs Frampton gave a derisive laugh. "Oh my, Margaret. What are you thinking of? I cannot use it now. It will be ruined."

Meg blushed, but she continued to press her point. "Not for you, Eugenia. For Sunday gowns for charity girls."

Peter saw the earnestness in her expression and feared her friend would disappoint her.

"What a splendid notion, don't you agree, Mr Barnes?" he said, drawing the curate into the conversation.

"I do, indeed. I can think of several charities which would welcome such a generous donation."

"As you wish," said Mrs Frampton with a condescending smile, "but I fear you'll be disappointed. I doubt the material will be salvageable, even to make dresses for poor girls, but if you believe it will suffice—"

"Thank you, Eugenia. I would hate to see it go to waste."

Though her smile didn't waver, her friend wrinkled her nose as if she had smelled something unpleasant. "Indeed."

From that point on, Mrs Frampton took command of the conversation, launching into a discussion of the King's illness, and her regret that he had stopped coming to Weymouth while she was still in the schoolroom.

As supper progressed, Peter noticed Meg grow increasingly quiet and once, she raised a hand to cover her mouth.

She coughed, but it didn't fool him. She had been stifling a yawn.

When they finished eating, they all returned to the ballroom together, and Mrs Frampton moved away to care for her other guests.

The curate took his leave, expressing his hope that he would see them in church the next day, and they both assured him of their intention of attending service on Christmas morning.

Peter was on the verge of asking Meg to dance with him again when he caught her trying to hide another yawn.

He chuckled to himself. Poor darling. She was not used to these late hours. "I think, perhaps, it is time for us to return home."

He knew he'd made the right decision when she didn't argue, but gave him a sleepy nod.

Ensconced inside Jethro's chaise, Peter was more aware of his proximity to Meg than he had been on the outward journey.

"Have you enjoyed yourself?"

She rubbed her eyes and nodded. "Very much so. And you?"

He paused before speaking, staring at the far side of the carriage. He wanted to tell her how he felt, but if he did, he would have to explain why he couldn't offer her more than his heart.

His stomach clenched at the thought.

But if they were going to have any chance of a future together, they had to be honest with each other. She needed to know the truth.

Please, God. Give me courage.

"I've had a wonderful evening. Because of you. I love you, Meg."

Silence. Had he made a mistake saying so much?

As he turned toward her, to see her expression, that he might better gauge her reaction, a rut in the road caused her to fall against him.

He waited for her to shift her position, but she didn't. Instead, she snorted in a most unladylike way.

Peter realised his declaration had gone unheard.

Meg was asleep.

He liked the feel of her warmth up against him and was in no hurry to push her away.

He pressed a kiss on her forehead. “Sleep well, my love.”

His confessions would have to wait for another day.

CHAPTER 18

Meg awoke with no clear idea of how the evening had ended. She had a hazy recollection of leaving the party and entering the carriage, but after that, just a sense of wellbeing only interrupted by the chill of the night air as she stumbled toward her front door, where Susan had received her and bundled her into bed.

She hugged her arms around herself. Yesterday, Peter had danced with her and now it was Christmas Day, and she would see him again. True, she would have to share him with his daughter and whoever else was at Miss Seymour's, but it would be the first time she'd spent a whole day in his company.

She would have liked to wear the sea-green dress which had drawn such warm praise from Peter the night before, but the ballgown was unsuitable for going to church. No. She would put on one of her other new dresses—the red sarcenet with long sleeves.

She pulled the bell rope, hoping Susan would not object to being summoned to help her get ready for the second day in a row, but she needed her assistance. That was the trouble with all the gowns Mrs Fisher had made for her. They fastened up the back, making them almost impossible to put on by yourself.

A few minutes later, the door of her bedchamber opened, and Susan appeared in the doorway, a jug in her hands and an unusually cheerful expression on her face.

She emptied the water into the bowl on the washstand and perched the jug on the table before enfolding Meg in a warm embrace. "A good morning to you, on this Christmas Day."

"By all appearances, a very good morning."

"Yes. It is. John has asked me to marry him."

"Oh, Susan. I'm so happy for you."

Her friend beamed from ear to ear. "He's going to talk to the curate after the service about having the banns read. Now he's finally had the courage to ask, he's as eager as anything to seal the knot. God willing, in three weeks' time, I'll be Mrs Pike. Now, get a move on, do. I don't want to keep John waiting."

While Meg sloshed water over her face, she pondered Susan's news. She was happy for her, but it would change things between them. And she couldn't help wondering whether the day would bring any alteration to her own prospects.

Peter had been very attentive at the ball. Was he just being the kind person he was, or did it mean something more?

As Susan fastened the ties of her friend's gown, she muttered under her breath. It brought a wry smile to Meg's lips. Her current blissful state didn't stop the grumbling.

"Out with it. How many more dresses did you order?"

Meg was loath to admit there was another evening gown and a walking dress still to arrive from Mrs Fisher's besides those already in her closet. She'd been persuaded to purchase rather more gowns than she should have, but Eugenia had insisted they were necessary, and so she had allowed herself to be swept along.

To judge by Mr Crowley's reaction to her appearance last night, it had been worth every shilling. But Susan's words made her feel uneasy. Was she suggesting they might not have enough money to pay for them?

She brushed the thought away, unwilling to think of that possibility now. Not with the prospect of a day in Peter's company before her.

"Tomorrow. We'll talk about it then."

"Very well. As it's Christmas."

Meg slipped her arms into her green spencer, pulled on the matching bonnet, and followed the others out of the front door. It was strange to see Susan blush when John tucked her arm firmly in his own.

She walked a little ahead of them along the seafront and down St Mary Street, trying to ignore the hollow feeling inside her, as she dwelt on her friend's happiness, whilst her own seemed yet out of reach. But maybe things were about to change for her, too.

When they entered the church, John held back while Meg took his place at Susan's side. Together, the two women walked up the aisle and sat down in Miss Whittaker's pew.

Meg suppressed a chuckle. Even now, she didn't regard the seat as hers. She would probably think of it as the old lady's pew for the rest of her life.

Moments later, Peter walked past, accompanied by his daughter and Mr Hunt. She could not resist glancing up at them and was rewarded by a nod from him and a wide grin from Annie.

Secure in the knowledge that she would be spending the day with them, Meg fixed her eyes on the picture of the Last Supper above the altar and turned her thoughts to worship.

After the service, she exited the church with Susan. As John approached them to claim his promised bride, Meg grasped her friend's hands and squeezed them.

"It will be strange not spending Christmas Day with you, as we've done for so many years, but I'm certain John will look after you."

"That he will. We'll be just fine. As for you, I'm sure you'll be enjoying yourself so much you won't spare us another thought."

Susan accompanied her words with a significant glance over her shoulder to where Mr Crowley and his daughter approached.

Meg pressed her lips together, unable to deny the accusation, as her friend released her hands, which were immediately grasped by Annie.

"I'm so pleased you're spending the day with us, Miss Harding. Just wait until you see the schoolroom. The tree is the best we've ever had."

Peter bowed toward her. "May I wish you a happy Christmas morn?"

"You may indeed. And the same to you."

They exchanged a few words with Mr Barnes, and then Peter offered her his arm as they walked to the school. There was no chance for serious conversation between them as Annie chattered all the way.

A servant took her spencer and hat and showed them into Miss Seymour's drawing room. Meg was taken aback to find it was such a well-appointed space. She had not expected a teacher's private apartments to show such taste.

It was more simply decorated than Eugenia's, but Meg preferred the less ostentatious style, and she thought it matched her hostess—reserved, but elegant.

Her gaze absorbed the festive scene. A huge log blazed in the grate. Greenery was spread along the mantelpiece, and some sprigs of holly with bright red berries were fixed above the doorway. But she couldn't spot any mistletoe. What a shame.

Meg turned to view the occupants of the room. Besides Miss Seymour, there were two other women and a tall lad of maybe ten or eleven years old.

The headteacher stepped forward to greet her.

"We're so pleased you could come, Miss Harding. Let me introduce you to the others. Joe, our foundling boy, who's become part of our family here at the school. One of my teachers, Miss Day, and Miss Lane, my housekeeper, who always joins us for our Christmas celebrations."

Meg curtseyed toward each woman in turn, and then perched on the edge of the sofa. Did she belong here any better than in Eugenia's ballroom?

She felt somewhat reassured when Peter sat down beside her, and Annie pulled up a chair.

"My, how pretty you look, Miss Harding. Don't you agree, Papa?"

"Pretty? I think not."

Meg saw the twinkle in Peter's eye and did not take offence, but his daughter gasped. "Papa! How can you be so rude?"

"Rude? To tell the truth?"

Her youthful face dropped. "But I thought..."

"Pretty is too insipid a word to describe Miss Harding's appearance. Her hair resembles burnished bronze and her dress is like rubies."

"Oh! That is much better than pretty," Annie said.

Meg agreed, and as Peter accompanied the compliment with a warmth-infused gaze, she dared to hope that today would see the fulfilment of her dreams.

The conversation became more general, and she sat listening to the others talk, offering the occasional comment, until dinner was announced.

She was relieved to find the food, though in plentiful supply, was not as sophisticated as the dishes served at Eugenia's party. Parsnip soup, roast beef, and goose. Mince pies and plum pudding.

Meg didn't think she'd ever eaten so well in her life.

Miss Seymour rose from her chair. "Let us adjourn to the schoolroom. Unless, of course, you wish to sit in solitary state over a glass of port, Mr Crowley?"

Peter laughed. "I'm happy to forego that pleasure—assuming Miss Lane has prepared her Wassail Bowl, as usual."

The housekeeper assured him she had, and they followed their hostess into a rectangular chamber Meg hadn't seen before. All the chairs had been pushed against the walls, leaving a large space clear in the middle. Greenery hung all around the room—garlands of holly and ivy and some branches of something which she thought might be juniper.

At one side stood a pianoforte, and at the other, on a table near the window, was the much talked about tree.

Meg stared at it, her mouth dropping open in wonder. The candles had been lit, and the bright light, mixed with the dark green of the yew, created a magical sight. Small paper cones full of sweetmeats hung from the branches and on the table beneath were two parcels.

"Admiring our handiwork?" Peter asked, coming alongside her.

"You and Annie did this? It's wonderful. Special—as Christmas should be. I'm surrounded by so much of my favourite colour. I adore evergreens. They remind me that some things never fade—like God's love. They give me hope that even in the most barren times, it is possible to thrive, and that spring will come again."

Peter took her hand and squeezed it. "I wish, one day—"

Meg held her breath, waiting for him to continue—but she didn't get to hear his wishes. He released his hold and broke off as Miss Seymour approached.

"You'll have to forgive me for entertaining in the schoolroom, Miss Harding. It's the only place in the house large enough for a dance."

Meg uttered a suitable response, and the headmistress moved away. She turned back to Peter for him to continue what he was saying, but he stood in silence, unable—or unwilling—to finish what he'd been about to tell her.

She shook off her disappointment and focused her mind on what Miss Seymour had said, which, when she thought about it, confused her.

"A dance? How is that to be contrived?" Meg whispered. "You're the only man here—unless you count Joe. Are we to take turns to partner you?"

Her words evoked Peter's deep chuckle. "I may be the only man now, but—ah, here they are."

Two gentlemen entered the room—Mr Barnes, the curate, and a stranger, whom Miss Seymour introduced as Mr Curtis, her solicitor.

The headmistress moved to the pianoforte and sat down. "Gentlemen, take your partners."

Mr Curtis frowned, giving Meg the distinct feeling the woman he wanted to dance with had chosen to play for them. But any sign of disappointment was gone in a flash and he turned to Peter's daughter and invited her to dance.

Annie blushed a deep shade of red as she grasped the solicitor's hand. Oh dear. It was obvious to Meg, if not to anybody else, that the girl was smitten with him.

To her relief, Mr Barnes claimed Miss Day as his partner, leaving Peter to stand up with her.

The dancing was far more enjoyable than at Eugenia's ball. No one minded if someone took a step wrong. There was nobody to impress. It was just friends together.

How she hoped these people would become *her* friends. She felt much more at ease with them than with Eugenia or her acquaintances.

As they took their seats after a lively reel, Annie said in a voice loud enough for all to hear, "Will I be allowed to dance at your party, Miss Harding?"

Meg sensed rather than observed everyone looking at her. How should she answer? If it were up to her, she would have no hesitation in letting Annie dance, but what would Eugenia think? She feared Mrs Frampton would be horrified if she permitted it.

"I...um..."

Peter recognised her difficulty and stepped in. "It wouldn't be proper for you to dance in public, Annie. Not until you're older."

"But Miss Harding is my friend. Why is it different from today?"

"There will be lots of other people at her party. People who will criticise her if she lets you dance. I'm not even sure you should be there."

Annie's bottom lip quivered, stirring Meg's compassion. It might be improper, but why should she hurt those she loved because she feared what others would say?

She wouldn't. What was the point of becoming a lady if it prevented her from following her own inclination? Perhaps she had set her sights too high.

Then her eyes fell on Peter. He was the reason she aspired to be a lady.

"I would like you all to come to my party on Twelfth Night," she said, looking around the room at the people she hoped would become her friends. "Including you, Annie. And if someone asks you to dance, and your father gives his permission, you need not hold back on my account."

The girl threw her arms around Meg and hugged her hard. "Thank you."

She held her close, revelling in the girl's affection, hoping she hadn't made a promise that would cost her dearly to keep. Would it deprive her of Eugenia's good opinion? Even of her friendship?

Meg brushed away the unpleasant thought. Why should she be weighed down by fear? It might never happen.

But it didn't stop her wishing that Peter would hold *her* tight, and tell her everything would be all right.

Chapter 19

It touched Peter that Meg cared about Annie's feelings. He wasn't sure he should allow it, but as his daughter had been given permission to attend the party on Twelfth Night, and even to dance, he knew he would not hear the end of it if he denied her this treat.

While they were dancing, Miss Lane had disappeared from the room. Now, she held the door open for a manservant carrying a huge bowl, which he placed on a side table set up for the purpose. A maid followed with a plentiful supply of glasses.

"Aha," he said to Meg. "Miss Lane's Wassail Bowl. You must try some."

Uncertainty clouded her eyes. "Will I enjoy it?"

He shrugged. "Taste it and find out."

They moved to the table where the housekeeper was ladling the ruby-coloured liquid into glasses. He handed a glassful to Annie and Miss Harding and accepted one for himself.

Peter's nose twitched with amusement as he watched Meg sip the drink as if she was afraid of it.

"Well? Do you like it?"

Her eyes sparkled as she licked her lips. "Very much so."

As she swallowed a larger gulp, she scrunched up her forehead. "What's in it?"

"Wine and some kind of spice and—"

He cast the housekeeper a helpless look, but she merely raised her eyebrows, an amused expression on her face.

"And I don't know what else, because Miss Lane guards her traditional family recipe closely."

"Oh, that's a shame. This is so delicious I'd love to make some for my party. Are you sure you can't divulge the ingredients, Miss Lane?"

"Despite what some people would have you believe," she replied, shooting Peter a good-humoured glare, "it's no secret what I put in my Wassail Bowl. Wine and spices, eggs, toast, and sugar, with roasted apples tossed in hissing hot, making it warm to drink. The skill is in the balance—and that's what I've honed over years of practice."

"And you won't share it?"

The woman laughed. "It's not that I won't share it. I can't. It is one thing to know what you must put into the Wassail Bowl, but quite another to be able to produce a blend with the right flavour. Every bottle of wine tastes slightly different, as does every batch of apples. I adjust the quantities of the other ingredients, so there's just the correct amount of sweetness. No two bowls ever taste precisely the same."

"I understand. My mama always used to say that the best cooking was done by taste, and if you didn't have a good tongue, you would never be a good cook."

"A wise woman, your mother," said Miss Lane, nodding her head in approval. "Did you often cook with her?"

"Occasionally, but not for many years—since I was a girl and went to live with Miss Whittaker."

"I didn't realise you'd been with her for so long," said Peter. "How old were you?"

"Twelve—and I haven't seen my mother since."

"Mama died when I was ten," said Annie, grasping her hand. "It's hard, isn't it? Not having a loving mother to guide you when you're growing up."

"Yes. It is."

Peter stared at Meg. Were those tears in her eyes? Were such memories still painful to her?

He needed to lighten the mood. To make her smile again. "Time for a game. What shall we play? Crambo? Speculation?"

They agreed upon charades and ensuring Meg was on his side, Peter divided them into two teams. Equipped with pencils and paper, they moved to opposite ends of the room.

"What word are we going to pick?" Mr Curtis asked.

Meg shrugged. "I don't know. Why do we even need a word?"

"Didn't you play games at Miss Whittaker's house?" Peter asked, shooting her a quizzical glance.

"A few—snapdragon and blind man's buff—but not this one. How does it work?"

"Each team composes a short poem to describe the word they've chosen, and the other team has to guess what it is," he explained. "We require a word with two parts, such as friendship or bridegroom or—"

"Honeymoon?" Her voice was full of innocence, but her green eyes twinkled up at him, and were accompanied by a wicked grin.

"Oh, yes. That will do very well," said Miss Lane, seemingly oblivious to the flirtatious undercurrent between him and Meg.

The housekeeper bent her head and wrote down a few words, and while Mr Curtis leaned over to see what she'd written, Peter pulled a face at Meg.

She responded with such a blinding smile that he would have thrown caution to the wind and taken her in his arms if they hadn't been in a roomful of people.

The poem complete, the two ladies insisted Peter read it out to the other team.

> "My first is as sweet as the cake on your plate.
> My second is sluggish and always up late.
> The whole is a journey I can't make with you
> Though it's never for one, but always for two."

By the amused smile on Miss Seymour's face, Peter assumed she had guessed the answer already, but the adults patiently encouraged the younger members of their team to work it out.

With a little help from her teachers, Annie solved the charade, and she clapped her hands in delight as she called out the solution.

"We've prepared our charade somewhat differently," said Miss Seymour. "Joe doesn't get on too well with words, so we're going to mime ours for you—think of it as a dumb charade."

Peter chuckled to himself as he watched Annie pretend to be queen, with Joe and the grown-ups bowing down before her. It was even more astonishing to see them act out the second part of the word, as they all fell to the ground together.

"I've got it!" Meg said, with almost as much enthusiasm as Annie. "Raindrop."

She met with no complaints when she suggested they play again with both teams miming. It proved so entertaining that the game kept them amused for a considerable time.

After singing carols around the pianoforte, Miss Seymour fetched the parcels from under the tree and gave one to each child.

Peter watched Annie open the delicate shell box she had received, and he heaved a sigh of relief when she squealed with delight at the necklace it contained.

"Miss Seymour made the box, so you can thank her for that, but the pearls are from me. They were your mother's, and I figured it was time you had them."

Annie thanked the teacher prettily, and then gave him a hug, exclaiming how pleased she was to receive her first grown-up piece of jewellery, and begging him to fasten it around her neck at once.

With her new finery in place, she paraded up and down the room to show off the pearls to the others.

"I think it's safe to say your daughter is pleased with her present," said Meg, coming up beside him.

Peter chuckled. "The funny thing is, nothing could highlight her childlikeness so successfully as her excitement at being given, what she calls, a proper necklace."

"Joe, on the other hand, is treating his box of toy soldiers with reverence," she said, nodding toward the corner of the room, where the boy had withdrawn with his treasure. He was picking up each one, and examining it fondly, his face lit with joy.

"Do you think Miss Seymour intends to encourage him to go into the army?"

He shrugged. "I don't know. God willing, the war will be over before he's of an age to join up."

Annie interrupted their conversation by insisting on a game of blind man's buff. Peter pressed his lips together, unsure how such a suggestion would be received. Was it his duty to discourage her from demanding they play the children's game, which he felt sure would be shunned in polite company?

Then he noticed the eagerness on Joe's face. He'd put down his box of toy soldiers to join in, and Peter couldn't bear to disappoint him.

"Just a few rounds then, Annie. Would you like to go first, Joe?"

Blindfolded, the boy stumbled around the room with his hands extended until he caught Mr Curtis in his grasp.

The solicitor took his turn and, to minimise the risk of embarrassing any of the ladies present, Peter ensured he was the next person to be taken prisoner.

The blindfold did not hinder Peter's aim to capture his daughter and end the game. It was easy to follow Annie around, as she squealed whenever he drew close. He almost caught her several times, but she kept darting away from him before he could catch her.

"Cheat! Cheat!" his daughter cried. "You're following me."

"And you're making so much noise, I could track you from the other side of Weymouth," Peter retorted.

Despite his warning, Annie continued to giggle, and he made a final lunge for her. However, at the last moment, she jumped out of the way, and he found someone else in his arms.

Everyone laughed and urged him to guess their identity.

He reached out and patted the top of his prisoner's head. To judge by their height, he'd captured a lady, and knowing his daughter's penchant for romance, he suspected Annie had ensured he'd caught Meg rather than one of the others.

Peter's breathing became laboured as he trailed his hands over his captive's curls and down the sides of her face.

There was no doubt. It was Meg.

He gulped hard as he traced the shape of her ears and nose, and ran a finger over her lips, making her catch her breath.

"You've had long enough. You have to guess now, Papa."

He rubbed his chin. "Hmm. My prisoner is definitely a lady, and not Annie, because her voice is coming from behind me. I believe the clue is in the hair. Only one lady present has curls—which means it must be Miss Harding. Am I correct?"

A round of applause confirmed he'd guessed right, and he pulled off the blindfold to find himself staring into Meg's eyes. Her cheeks were flushed a becoming pink, and not the deep red he half expected to see. To his relief, there was no suggestion she was unduly perturbed or embarrassed.

"I hope you're satisfied, Annie, that we've played the game you chose."

His daughter pouted. "But I haven't had a go yet."

"We've played enough for tonight."

Meg grabbed the blindfold from his hand and grinned. "My turn, I believe."

"It's not necessary for you—"

"Are you trying to deprive me of my revenge, Mr Crowley?"

"As you wish."

He fastened the scarf on her head and spun her three times.

She blundered about, holding her palms in front of her to feel her way.

His daughter was as noisy as before, but it was him Meg trailed around the room, not her. Peter held his breath as she cornered him by the pianoforte.

"Which way's Annie?" she said, so quietly only he could hear.

How did she know it was him? Still, it was a relief to think she didn't intend to catch him.

Just the thought of her running her hands over his face was enough to send his pulse racing. He wasn't sure he'd be able to resist kissing her fingers if she traced his mouth in the same way he'd done to her.

"To your left," he whispered back.

Meg took a step forward, as if she were going to capture him, and at the last moment, she veered toward his daughter and caught her in her grasp.

"Now, who could this be?" she said, tickling her prisoner under the chin so she squealed.

"I would recognise that noise anywhere. You give yourself away, Miss Crowley."

Everyone clapped and Meg removed the blindfold. "I will have to get my revenge on your father on another occasion."

Miss Seymour declared it was time for refreshments, and rang for tea and coffee to be brought into the schoolroom, along with a fresh supply of mince pies.

As the clock struck midnight, the two other gentlemen took their leave, signalling the breakup of the party.

"Come, Annie," said Miss Seymour, in what Peter considered her teacher's voice. "Time for you to bid your father goodnight and retire to bed."

"Yes, madam."

"I'll give you a few minutes together."

Miss Seymour and her staff left the room, leaving Peter alone with the two most important females in his life.

Annie hugged Meg and then turned and pecked his cheek.

"I will give *you* a few minutes alone. Goodnight, Papa."

She skipped out of the door, beaming from ear to ear, clearly rather pleased with herself.

He turned to Meg and grimaced. "I'm sorry."

"For what? If you're apologising for being left alone with me, I'll be most upset."

Peter closed the distance between them. "I'm not sorry for that—but I'm not sure it's wise."

"Oh? And why's that, Mr Crowley?"

"Because I'm not certain I trust myself with you."

He wanted to kiss her. Claim her as his own.

Why should he care what others thought of him? He would take Meg without her house, but the building would certainly make it easier to look after her and his daughter.

Did it matter that his future was uncertain? If she loved him as he loved her, surely, with God's help, they could figure it out together.

His mind was made up. He would not wait until his life was perfect. He would surge ahead now and ask her to marry him.

But first, he would kiss her.

Peter captured one of her hands and led her to the far end of the schoolroom. Opposite the pianoforte, over the doorway to the left, he'd hung a lone sprig of mistletoe, hoping he would have the opportunity to use it.

The entrance was recessed, so the white-berried foliage was hidden from the rest of the room until you were almost under it.

When Meg saw it, she gasped.

Peter dropped her hand, giving her the option to escape, but she didn't. Her face turned up to his in expectation, and his breath caught at the trust he saw.

He lowered his lips to hers, touching them gently, savouring the velvety feel of her mouth, before pulling away.

He gazed into her eyes, searching for the words to describe how much he loved her. To ask her to marry him. But before he could do that, he needed to tell her the truth.

"Meg, I—"

She reached an arm around his neck and pulled him down again, cutting off his words as she pressed her mouth to his in a demanding kiss that took his breath away.

"I knew it. I knew it," Annie said, squealing with delight, as she hurried over to them.

Meg sighed at the same moment as Peter, and they both chuckled. "Perfect timing as ever."

He leaned toward Meg. "We'll finish this conversation later. My work will keep me busy this week, but walk out with me on Sunday after the service."

He cast a meaningful look in his daughter's direction. "Perhaps, that way, we can contrive for a little privacy. There are things that need to be said for which I want an audience of one."

"I know," she whispered.

But Peter knew she didn't.

There were things he must say before he could offer his hand—things that might make her view his proposal in a different light.

Chapter 20

The following week dragged. Meg longed for Sunday when her hopes would be realised.

Peter had promised to finish the conversation he had started under the mistletoe, and after their kiss, she knew how it would end.

He would ask her to marry him—and she would say yes.

A sliver of guilt wormed its way into her thinking and niggled at her insides, disturbing her blissful anticipation of a rosy future.

Would she interrupt him if he tried to propose? To tell him the truth. That she was nothing more than a servant who had been fortunate enough to be left a house by her employer. And a small sum of money. Much smaller than everyone seemed to think.

The recollection of that small sum of money brought another unwelcome thought to her mind. She had promised to listen to Susan's remonstrances, once Christmastide was over.

What a relief that by that time she would be betrothed to Peter, and could pass over all her financial concerns to him.

There was a single knock on her door. Susan entered the room and stood in front of the bed, hands on her hips, with a scowl that would turn the milk sour.

"Get up. We need to talk."

"If you're going to growl at me like that, I'd rather stay here," Meg replied, pulling the sheets over her head.

"I meant to wait until after your party to talk about money, but things have come to a crisis, and we can't delay any longer."

With an unceremonious yank at her bedcovers, Susan exposed her to the morning chill.

"I'll have the conversation with you right here if you won't stir yourself, but I'd rather have it in the kitchen, with a pot of tea to hand."

Meg grunted her agreement and scrambled out of bed to dress and join her friend in the kitchen.

After pouring two cups of tea, Susan threw a piece of paper down on the table in front of her. "Explain this, if you please."

Meg picked up the sheet. It was a neatly written statement of account from Mrs Fisher listing the various gowns and other items the dressmaker had supplied, together with how much each cost. The total was so staggering that her eyes grew wide in disbelief.

"So much? How is that possible?"

Susan's mouth tightened. "My question exactly."

"I knew Mrs Fisher's dresses were not cheap, but Eugenia said it was better to buy quality—"

"Spare me Mrs Frampton's wisdom. She has more money than she knows what to do with. I warned you of the dangers of stepping outside your own circle."

She dropped a pile of bills on top of the dressmaker's account. "I suppose we have your frivolous friend to thank for these as well."

As Meg picked up each one and looked at the sum demanded, her unease grew. She knew she'd spent quite a lot of money, but she hadn't realised just how much.

"Is that the total amount?" Susan asked. "I'd rather know the worst all at once."

"Nothing worth talking about that I can recall."

"Are you sure? What about those?" she asked, pointing at Meg's feet.

"Haven't we paid the shoemaker already?"

"No."

"I don't understand. I bought these shoes two weeks ago. Hasn't the bill arrived yet?"

"More credit?"

"Eugenia told me—"

"What did the wretched woman say this time?"

Meg shuddered at the bitterness in her voice. It was clear Susan had no small dislike of Mrs Frampton. Was she jealous?

"Eugenia laughed at my ignorance and informed me that was the way things were done. There was no difficulty in setting up an account when she offered to vouch for me."

The ominous expression on Susan's face made her quake, and she dropped her gaze to her lap to avoid witnessing the condemnation in her eyes.

She forced herself to ask the question which plagued her mind, although she feared the answer. "Have we...can we...pay them?"

"Yes—and no."

She glanced up at the strange reply. "What do you mean?"

"It's possible for us to settle this bill—but not out of this quarter's income. We'll need to withdraw some of the capital. I'm not certain quite how much. But it means we'll have less money to live on next quarter, and every quarter after that."

The consequences of her folly hit Meg hard. "So, we'll have to make drastic economies to keep ourselves warm and well fed?"

Susan nodded.

"I'm sorry. I got caught up in the excitement of having an income of my own and thought it seemed like a fortune."

"And you were busy trying to impress Mr Crowley."

Heat rushed to Meg's cheeks. "Yes."

"Have you succeeded?"

Meg squirmed in her seat. "I think so—but he's not yet aware of the truth about me. That I was Miss Whittaker's maid, not her companion. He still thinks I'm some relative of the old lady's."

"Ah. So it will all come to nothing, as I predicted."

"Or Peter will rescue us."

"With what? Has he some secret pot of money I don't know about? Last I heard, he was working for that Lord Barnes, and from what I've gathered from the gossip flying around the market, he'll be fortunate if it lasts. Quite a temper, his lordship has, and if your Mr Crowley gets on the wrong side of it—"

"Then he'll get another position. But that's not what I meant. Neither you nor I have been brought up to deal with money, but he's a man. He'll be able to take care of us."

"Of you," Susan said in a peevish voice. "What's going to happen to John and me if you marry him? Our fates will be in his hands, not yours. Miss Whittaker didn't leave her house to me."

"You'll always have a home here. Both of you. I promise."

Susan sniffed hard. "Thank you. I appreciate that, but whether or not Mr Crowley proposes, that doesn't get us out of this mess. Mrs Fisher and the others still need to be paid. These are good people who work for a living. If we don't pay, they suffer."

Shame weighed on Meg's heart. Ignoring every prick of her conscience, she had followed a dream, and as a result, she had nearly ruined them. Eugenia had swept her along, encouraging her to spend money she couldn't afford.

Worse than that, she had excused her behaviour by telling herself she must have these things to be acceptable to her new friend.

And to attract Peter.

What a fool she'd been. If he desired her to be someone she wasn't, she should have discovered that earlier—before she had fallen in love with him.

The truth was long overdue and she wouldn't delay any longer. If he couldn't accept her as she was, so be it.

Her heart would shatter, but she would know she had done the correct thing. It was impossible to keep living a lie and trying to justify it to herself.

Lord, forgive me, and help me put things right.

A wave of something akin to peace flooded her being, refreshing her spirits and lightening her mood. The matter was far from resolved, but she discovered, to her surprise, what a relief it was to stop pretending she was someone she wasn't. She hadn't realised how exhausting it had been.

Besides, it wasn't as if it were an option any more. Her extravagance had made sure of that.

Meg drained her cup of lukewarm tea and took a deep breath.

"There is no question of not paying our bills. No one else must suffer for my mistakes—including you. Tell me how much money we need, and I'll arrange to withdraw it. And I promise I won't be ashamed of my humble beginnings anymore. In the future, if you catch me trying to be someone I'm not, you have my full permission to remind me of this moment."

"It's a relief to hear you say that. Now, I believe we have a chance to recover. God willing, we'll muddle through."

Susan hesitated. "What about your party with all your fancy friends?"

"That's one way I can save money. I'll visit Eugenia and explain the situation. Tell her I need to cancel the entertainment. I expect it will be the end of our friendship, but maybe that's not such a bad thing."

Susan promised she'd tally the figures on the bills to work out the total of their debts.

Meg thanked her and rose to fetch her pelisse and hat. Faced with disaster, losing her Twelfth Night celebration seemed trivial, but informing Mrs Frampton of her decision was another matter.

She needed to visit Eugenia before her courage deserted her.

But it wasn't the fear of her friend's disdain that bothered her the most.

What would Peter think of her when he discovered she wasn't the lady of quality he thought she was?

Chapter 21

Meg's spirits sank when she arrived at Eugenia's house to discover she was not alone. In her eagerness to cancel the party while there was still time, she had forgotten her friend had guests staying. There were three other women in the drawing room, none of whom she knew.

Eugenia was pleasant enough, begging her to join them, and trying to draw her into the conversation, but they talked on subjects on which she had little to say, so her contribution to the discussion was minimal.

At length, one of the ladies suggested they take a walk along the seafront.

Meg saw a chance to grab a few quiet words with Eugenia and hastened to encourage the idea. "As long as your pelisse and hat are thick enough to protect you from the cold, you'll find no complaint with the weather. The wind is light, and the sun is shining. It's a perfect day for a winter's walk by the sea."

The notion took root and, dressed in warm outer garments, they walked along the seafront toward town. Much to Meg's dismay, the ladies formed a single group, and she was obliged to resort to retying the lace of her half-boot to isolate Eugenia from the rest.

Fortunately, her friend was too polite to leave her alone, though her frequent glances after the other three women betrayed her desire to be with her guests.

Summoning up her courage Meg addressed Eugenia. "I must speak with you on a matter of some urgency."

"Oh?"

"It's about my party next week."

"I am so looking forward to it. Alas, I fear Mr Frampton will not return from his business trip in time to accompany me, but—"

"Stop."

Eugenia halted her steps and stared at Meg in some alarm. "Are you ill?"

"No, indeed. I'm quite well, but I can't let you continue. I'm sorry to disappoint you, but I must cancel the party."

Eugenia's eyebrows shot up so high they met her hairline. "Impossible."

Meg blinked in surprise. Of all the possible reactions to her announcement she had considered, that was not one of them.

"I cannot allow it," her friend continued, linking arms as they resumed their promenade. "The invitations have gone out, and I've promised my guests a dance. What reason can you have to suggest such a thing?"

This was the moment Meg dreaded. "I've been too free with my spending, and if I don't retrench, I will come to an abrupt halt."

"Pshaw! Is that all that ails you? I suppose Mrs Fisher is pushing for payment of her account."

"Yes, her bill has arrived and—"

"Oh, if you've only just received it, you can delay a month or two, at least."

"But the debt is due now."

"That may be what she says, but it's not what she expects. She won't anticipate you paying her immediately. Nobody does. Order another dress. That's what I do if I've overspent my allowance. Relieves me of needing to ask Mr Frampton for more money."

"I beg your pardon. How does buying an additional gown help the situation? It just increases the amount you owe."

"Yes, but by the time that bill becomes due, it will be a new quarter, and I'll be able to settle the whole debt in one go."

If that was the way Eugenia paid her bills, Meg wondered that any of the tradesmen in town let her run up an account. How did they survive if the gap between supplying goods and receiving payment for them was so large?

She didn't know, but she was determined not to add to the problem. She refused to follow Eugenia's example.

"I am not prepared to do that. I must cancel the party."

"No. You must not. I could not tolerate you being ridiculed by my guests. What excuse could I give them if you refuse to go ahead? I can hardly tell them you've run out of money. They would laugh and wonder at your strange notions."

Meg was unmoved. "I am sorry to provoke their scorn, but I'll have to bear it as well as I can."

"But what about me?" Eugenia asked, brushing her eye with a glove. "If you won't change your mind to protect yourself, think of how your actions will reflect on me. My guests will accuse me of having poor taste in friends. How could you treat me so carelessly?"

She sniffed and wiped away another tear.

Guilt tore at Meg's heart. Eugenia was crying. It had not occurred to her that her friend would lose face if she cancelled her Twelfth Night party. "I'm sorry, I didn't think..."

"Then you'll change your mind? What would it cost you to feed thirty or forty guests and entertain them with a little music? Hardly anything compared to the price of one of Mrs Fisher's gowns. Please, Margaret. You wouldn't be so cruel as to let me down."

Meg thought of her rash declaration to Susan just a few hours before. She had asserted that her mistakes would hurt nobody, but if she refused to change her mind, Eugenia would be humiliated—and it would be her fault.

"I'll see what can be contrived."

Eugenia's countenance transformed in an instant. "I knew you'd come to your senses. A modicum of discomfort now will be worth it. Trust me."

Meg pasted a false smile on her lips and left the ladies to continue their promenade without her.

As she walked toward her house, the sinking feeling in her stomach grew as two questions consumed her mind.

How was she going to pay for the party?

And how would she tell Susan?

Chapter 22

Full of hope, Peter rode out to Lord Barnes's estate. Tomorrow was Sunday. He would see Meg and put his future into her hands.

Regardless of how others might view his actions, he would abandon caution and ask her to marry him. So what if they deemed him a fortune hunter? If his bride did not object, neither would he.

When he arrived, the butler opened the door to him, but failed to respond to his cheerful greeting.

Peter stared at him. He appeared somewhat strained around the eyes. Had he endured a sleepless night?

He was about to make his way to his office when the man spoke. "Lord Barnes wishes to speak with you in his study."

That was a surprise. He hadn't expected his employer's return for another week, as the weather was so fine.

"Oh? When did he arrive?"

"Late last night, sir."

"Very well. I'll just fetch a notebook—"

"You're to go to his room straightaway. His lordship was most insistent."

Peter heaved a sigh. That would explain the butler's haggard expression. Both Jethro and Mr Barnes had warned him of the baron's temper, and if he was in a foul mood, it would not be wise to delay.

He hoped his employer hadn't found reason to complain of his work after only being home for a few hours.

Peter knocked on the door of Lord Barnes's study and waited for him to reply, but there was no answer. Perhaps the butler had mistaken the urgency of his summons.

He was about to knock again when the door was pulled open from the inside, not by the baron, but by Mr Barnes.

The curate's father did not rise from his seat. He wrinkled his nose as if an unpleasant smell had entered the room with him. That didn't augur well.

"So, you have appeared at last."

"I had no notion you'd returned and required my presence earlier."

"Huh! Sit."

Peter obeyed and waited to hear what his lordship had to say.

Mr Barnes hovered by the door. "I'll bid you a good day, Father."

"No. I want you to stay, Gilbert."

"As you wish." He shot Peter an apologetic glance as he sat down in the other chair.

"I have just returned from my brother's house in Salisbury. A visit, I might add, I was obliged to cut short, because I learned some very disturbing information."

He glared at him. "Well? What have you got to say for yourself?"

An icy chill fell on Peter, trickling down his body from the top of his head to the tips of his toes. He had a nasty suspicion he knew what the baron was alluding to, but he could not respond when he didn't know what his lordship had learned.

"You wish me to spell it out, do you? Whilst I was in Salisbury, my path crossed with that of your old employer—and his wife. Ah, no wonder you pale at my words. It always puzzled me why he'd supplied you with such a brief reference, but now I know. I made the mistake of boasting to Mrs Elsworth how useful you were to me, and how glad I was you'd decided to leave them. Which is when I learned what really happened. That you had been dismissed. Without notice."

Out of the corner of his eye, Peter could see the concern on the curate's face.

"Still nothing to say in your defence? Do you deny it?"

"I cannot deny the facts."

He heard a sharp intake of breath beside him and threw Mr Barnes a rueful grimace.

"Save your shock for the sordid truth, Gilbert. Mrs Elsworth told me her husband had dismissed this man for misconduct—with a lady."

The curate leaped to his feet. "I don't believe it."

Peter warmed to hear himself so valiantly championed, but the baron's words made him feel sick to the bottom of his stomach. Just what had she told him?

Lord Barnes shook his head at his son, a rather superior look on his face. "Sit down. There is no need for this show of emotion. It is quite uncalled for."

Once Mr Barnes had retaken his seat, his father spoke again, his tone growing more patronising.

"I hate to disillusion you, Gilbert, but you must remember this is not mere speculation. Mrs Elsworth told me this herself. She said her husband wouldn't keep this man in his employ another day after what had happened. That though his work was exemplary, his behaviour was... regrettable. She was disappointed in you, Crowley. Very disappointed. Would you care to explain yourself?"

The baron raised his eyebrows, but Peter remained silent. If Mrs Elsworth had given his lordship no details, then neither would he.

"Speak, man—or must I speak for you? I told her I would keep her counsel, but I want you to hear this, Gilbert. It is your duty as a clergyman—"

"End right there, Father. If you promised Mrs Elsworth your discretion, then be true to your word. It would be wise not to cast a slur on a lady's reputation."

His lordship's colour rose. "You are a man of the cloth, and this cad is the culprit. I insist you listen—"

"No. Stop. If Mr Crowley chooses to confess his sins to me, so be it. He is one of my parishioners, and I cannot refuse him that relief. You would do well to keep your promise to Mrs Elsworth. It is enough that you know."

"Have it your way! But take heed. The truth has a habit of coming out."

Lord Barnes snarled at Peter. "Get out of here—and don't expect a recommendation from me. I'll not let you wreak havoc in some other poor, unsuspecting man's household."

Peter's chest tightened. "I see. Won't you even supply me with a terse reference like Mr Elsworth's?"

"I will not."

"Very well, then I would be obliged if you would return his recommendation to me."

His lordship ruffled amongst the papers in front of him until he found the brief letter from Peter's previous employer.

With a sneer on his face, the baron tore up the paper, rose from his desk, and tossed the pieces in the fire. "Does that answer your question?"

The icy chill that had entered Peter's body when he realised his past had caught up with him now seeped deeper, freezing his heart.

He was being turned off with no reference, just after the quarter day.

Lord Barnes had dashed all his hopes with a single swipe of his hand.

Peter knew his prospects of getting another position were slim. No one would take him on as steward without a recommendation, and the outlook would be even worse if the baron divulged what Mrs Elsworth had told him, which he would have done today if his son had not prevented it.

The truth about his dismissal would not, he feared, stay a secret for long.

The worst of it was that he couldn't defend himself without breaking his word to the man who had employed him for so many years. Though Mr Elsworth had refused to believe his story, he had sworn him to silence.

It was a promise Peter felt honour-bound to keep, but he hadn't realised how dearly it would cost him.

He rose to leave, his feet as heavy as lead, and his heart even heavier.

Mr Barnes—God bless him—extended his arm and shook hands with him, despite the scowl on his father's face.

But the curate was powerless to plead Peter's case. As powerless as Peter was himself.

It was his word against another's, just like before.

Mr Elsworth had lost faith in Peter's integrity, and so had Lord Barnes.

And they both believed he was guilty.

Chapter 23

Peter trudged over the fields, the cold inside him matched by the chill of the wind, the journey home taking far longer, as Lord Barnes had reclaimed his horse.

How could his life have changed so much in a single day? Only that morning, he had been full of hope for the future, but now his dreams lay shattered.

He dreaded the thought of the morrow's meeting with Meg, which he had looked forward to so eagerly.

His dismissal from Mr Elsworth's had been painful, but this was excruciating. Bound as he was by his promise to his old employer, he couldn't tell Meg the whole story.

He had been so convinced that God had used that turn of events—though bad in itself—to bring him to Weymouth.

To be with the woman he loved.

But not anymore. She was being torn from him, and somehow, it was worse than when he had lost his wife, because Meg was alive—waiting for him, expecting him to propose. And he must disappoint her.

Because in all good conscience, he could no longer ask her to marry him.

By the time he reached Weymouth, he had talked himself into a melancholy.

As he passed the turnpike gate, Peter balled his right hand into a fist and rammed it into his left palm with a satisfying smack.

What was he going to do? He could never wed Meg now. *Smack.* He could get work as a labourer, but he wouldn't earn enough to pay Annie's school fees. *Smack.* And where would they live? He couldn't stay with Jethro forever. *Smack.*

Perhaps his friend would employ him as a footman. But Annie...?

His fist hovered in the air, and then flopped to his side, his gut twisting at the fear that his daughter might be obliged to find work, rather than finish her education.

Please, Lord. Not that.

After a restless night, Peter braced himself for the painful interview with Meg that he was determined to have straight after the church service. If he put it off any longer, he reckoned he might expire.

His thoughts were not on worship as he walked into St Mary's that morning. He gazed around the building, searching for Meg's beloved face, but she wasn't there.

His mind kept drifting as he uttered the liturgical responses that were so familiar to him.

Where was Miss Harding? Was she ill? Had she learned of his disgraceful dismissal? Was she trying to avoid him?

At last, Mr Barnes spoke the final blessing. It took all Peter's self-control not to run from the pew, though why he was so desperate to see Meg, when his visit could only bring disappointment, he couldn't rightly say.

As Peter neared Meg's house, his steps slowed. How different it was from the last time he had walked along the Esplanade by the sea with her.

He knocked on the front door, bracing himself for what was to come, and the usual manservant answered.

"Is Miss Harding at home to visitors?"

It came as no surprise when the man said nothing, as Peter had grown accustomed to his peculiar ways, but instead of welcoming him inside, the servant tried to shut him out.

On instinct, he stuck out his foot to prevent the door from closing.

"I need to speak to Miss Harding."

"You can't."

The man again attempted to close the door, but Peter kept his boot against the wood.

"A moment, if you please. When do you expect your mistress to return?"

"She's not out—but you can't see her."

He refused to give up. "Is she ill?"

The servant puckered his brow as if puzzled how to answer and heaved a sigh of relief when Meg's maid came to stand beside him.

The woman pursed her lips, glaring at the seemingly unwanted visitor, as if trying to decide what to do. After a few moments, she spoke.

"It's fine, John. Let him in."

The man moved away from the door so fast that Peter half-fell into the hallway. When he recovered his footing, he found the woman staring at him again.

"I hope I'm doing the right thing," she muttered to herself, before bidding him to follow.

To his surprise, she led him down a flight of stairs to the servants' quarters, and showed him into the kitchen.

A lone figure sat hunched over the table, her head in her hands, and the sound of heart-wrenching sobs filled the room.

All Peter's noble plans of breaking the news gently fled. Every instinct urged him to comfort Meg. She must have heard of his disgrace, and she was devastated.

He sat down on the bench and put his arm around her. She lifted her gaze, and when she saw it was him, she rested her head on his shoulder and sobbed even more.

Peter let her cry until her tears ran out, his own eyes moist at the sight of her distress. His conscience smote him that nothing he could say would ease her pain. What he'd come to tell her would only increase it.

When the sobbing stilled to the occasional wavering sniff, he withdrew his arm to extract a clean handkerchief from his pocket, which he offered to her.

Despite the temptation, he did not resume his comfortable position with his arm draped around her shoulder, but pulled away a little. If he stayed in such proximity to Meg, he would end up kissing her, and that would not be fair. Not when he couldn't offer what she wanted.

"Can you tell me why you're so upset?" he whispered, though he dreaded her answer, fearing he had caused her distress.

She blew her nose and held the handkerchief in her lap as she spoke. "I've not been honest with you."

The unexpected words made Peter blink with astonishment.

"I am not who you think I am—and I can't hide it any longer."

His heart stilled. What dreadful secret was she about to reveal? God forbid—was she married?

"Everyone thinks I'm Miss Whittaker's niece, but I'm not."

He let out a whoosh of relief. "I know that. You told me so yourself."

"But I failed to make you understand that I'm not related to her at all. I was never more than a servant in her household."

"You undervalue yourself. A companion is superior to a servant—"

"But I wasn't her companion—just her lady's maid. I travelled with her because there was no one else. You pitied me because you thought I was a lady who'd come down in the world, but for a girl who started off in the kitchens, I was blessed indeed to have risen to such a height.

"It was a complete surprise to discover Miss Whittaker had left me this house and enough money to live on. If only I'd kept to my original plan for a simple life, I wouldn't be in this muddle, but when I met you again, I so wanted to be worthy of your regard that I got carried away by my dreams and I've spent too much on hats and dresses and I don't know how we'll survive or how I'm going to pay for a party that won't put Eugenia to the blush or—"

Meg broke off and stared up into his face. Peter guessed she saw the agony building inside him. He wanted to enfold her in his arms and assure her he didn't care about her background.

But he couldn't.

The disgrace he was facing was his burden to bear. He would keep trusting that God would work things out, but until then, he must face it alone.

"I can see it in your gaze. You're not going to finish the conversation we had on Christmas Day, are you?" she said in a small voice so laced with sadness that it tugged at his heartstrings.

"I can't."

Meg sniffed hard. "Then my dreams were just that—dreams—and I was foolish to run after them. I have the satisfaction of knowing that my current plight is my own fault, and it was all for nought. I thought—I hoped—you could see beyond what I was..."

She stared up at him, her eyes so wide and desolate that it wrung his heart.

And there was nothing he could do about it.

Chapter 24

Meg chided herself for being such a fool. She had known from the first Peter would never marry someone like her, but she'd deceived herself into thinking their mutual affection had created something more solid between them.

She'd told him the truth about her humble beginnings, and her hope was revealed for what it was—a castle of dreams, built on the sand, and now the tide had come in and it had tumbled down, washed away by the sea.

Why hadn't she concentrated on doing what was right, being honest with Peter instead of giving into vanity and ambition? Then at least she would not have blamed herself for her misery, and that knowledge must have lessened the heartache and regret that now consumed her.

Forgive me, Lord.

Peter jerked Meg out of her self-recriminations by jolting the bench in his hurry to rise from his seat. For some minutes he paced up and down the kitchen, but at length, he stopped before her and spoke.

"I should probably keep my mouth shut, for nothing is further from my wishes than to cause you more pain, but I cannot have you think so poorly of me. Do you imagine the depth of my love is so shallow that I would withhold the offer of my hand because of discovering you began life as a servant?"

"It's only to be expected. I'm sure most gentlemen would act that way."

"But do you believe it of me?"

Did she? She hadn't once, but now? Meg didn't know what to believe anymore. "I don't think you would give me up because of what I revealed if your affections were truly engaged. I can only assume they aren't. Perhaps the kiss, which meant so much to me, showed you the state of your own heart, and you've been deluding yourself that you loved me."

"That's not true."

Now it was Meg's turn to jump up from her place on the bench. She didn't know whether she was on her head or her heels. What was she supposed to think?

Peter claimed to hold her in affection, and yet he would not, or could not, marry her. Should she rejoice in the assurance of his regard or cry from the pain of her shattered hopes?

She glared up at his face. "I don't understand. You declare you love me and are unaffected by what I have revealed about my past, and yet you will not finish the conversation we began on Christmas Day. If you want me to believe you love me, tell me why?"

His shoulders slumped as he exhaled deeply. "Something from *my* past has caught up with me. I didn't leave my previous position—I was dismissed. A few days ago, Lord Barnes learned what happened, and he's dismissed me, too."

Her jaw dropped open. What crime had he committed that had persuaded not one, but two employers to dismiss him? She had to know. "And what *did* happen?"

After a long pause, Peter spoke again, but he wouldn't meet her eyes. "There was a scandal. Involving a lady. My employer refused to believe in my innocence. And now there are consequences from which I cannot escape."

Meg's lower lip trembled. How naïve she'd been.

Despite his handsome appearance, it had never occurred to her there was another lady in his life. One who still had some hold over him—a claim to his hand, if not his love.

She had heard too much gossip in the servants' hall not to know that gentlemen didn't always behave properly toward women. She had thought Peter better than that, and it pained her to acknowledge this dent in his character, but though it hurt, Meg applauded his decision to do right by this woman, whoever she was, and she would not stand in his way.

"And now you find you cannot follow your heart?" she whispered.

He closed his eyes and nodded.

"So be it. It is some comfort to know you care for me."

For a long moment, Meg stared at his woebegone face, which seemed to match the sorrow she felt deep inside. Where she must bury it, along with her love.

There was no point dwelling on what could not be. She should have known it would not last.

Peter drew his brows together and thrust out his right hand toward her. "May we still be friends?"

Without pausing to think, Meg grasped it, revelling in the feel of his touch—though she knew she shouldn't—and shook it warmly. "I should like that."

The corners of Peter's mouth turned up. "I feared you would hate me."

"I could never hate you. If all you can offer me is friendship, I accept. I could do with a friend I trust just now."

"You still trust me?" he asked incredulously.

"Is there any reason I shouldn't?"

"No, but—"

"I won't pretend that I wish the circumstances were different, but you're acting honourably, and I wouldn't have it any other way. You must not fear that I shall try to change your mind."

"I am forever in your debt, Meg. You have taught me to love again."

His words reinforced the wretchedness of her position and stirred up the feelings she was trying to repress. The hollowness in her heart was spreading so fast it threatened to engulf her—and she felt powerless to resist.

"Then you did not love her?" Meg asked, before she could stop herself.

Peter shuddered. "No. She—"

"I don't need to know."

"I wish I could defend myself."

"Would it alter anything?"

An agonised look passed over his face. "No."

The pain in his expression called to something deep within Meg's soul. She could not be strong for herself, but with God's help, she would be brave for him.

And though he could not marry her, perhaps he would still come to her rescue.

"Then let's put what might have been aside and say no more about it, and let me call on your support as a friend. You have far more experience of life than I have. Please help me, if you can. What in heaven's name am I supposed to do to get out of the mess I'm in?"

"Will you be open with me? Just how bad have things got?"

Meg gestured toward the sheaf of bills and other papers on the table. She picked up the top one and handed it to him. "These are Susan's calculations. You must pardon any errors. She's not accustomed to such large sums."

"Susan isn't your lady's maid, is she?"

"No. She was Miss Whittaker's cook. The amounts she's used to dealing with are for vegetables and cuts of meat."

His eyes grew wide as he stared at the figures on the sheet in front of him. "Did you really spend this much on a few gowns?"

The heat rushed into Meg's face. "Eugenia assured me it was money well spent. You complimented me when I wore them."

Peter grimaced. "I admired you when you were wearing shabby black dresses and worked for Miss Whittaker. Did you truly think these trimmings were necessary to attract my interest?"

"I wanted to be your equal."

"Huh! I thought you were above me, in fortune, if not in status."

He continued to peruse the pile of bills. Taking a pencil from his pocket, he wrote some figures on the page next to Susan's.

"I'm sorry, Meg. Once you pay these bills out of your capital, your income will be so small that you'll have no recourse but to sell the house."

She stifled a sob, biting down on her lip in distress. It was even worse than she feared. "Is there no other way? I'll go back into service to cover the cost of heating the house until I've saved up enough—"

"You've no notion about money at all, have you? Your wages as a maid couldn't repair the shortfall in income you face."

"They couldn't?"

"No."

"Then we'll have to sell the house and get somewhere smaller, and I'll have to hope that one day Susan will forgive me for my extravagance and for letting her and John down."

Peter reached out and squeezed her hand, but she snatched it away.

"I don't deserve your sympathy. I've brought this on myself. But I'm determined not to let anyone else suffer for my mistakes, if I can prevent it. Despite the perilous nature of my finances, I have to hold my Twelfth Night party as planned."

"Please don't do so on Annie's account. I'll make your excuses."

"I would hate to disappoint your daughter, but it's for Mrs Frampton's sake I must go ahead with it."

"Does her good opinion matter so much that you'd run up more debts to secure it?"

Meg winced at the accusatory tone of his voice and wavered in her decision. Should she cancel the party after all? But then she remembered the tears in Eugenia's eyes when she had suggested that course of action and resolved not to cause her friend further distress.

"I can't forget how kindly she befriended me, when I first came to Weymouth—"

"And persuaded you to spend more than you should have."

"She meant well, Peter. It's not her fault I've run up bills I can't afford to pay. I owe her this much—to save her from the derision of her friends, if possible, by holding my party in a style that won't embarrass her, though how it is to be contrived when the coffers are empty, I don't know."

"Very well, seeing as you're so determined, I'll do what I can to help. Where do you intend to entertain your guests?"

"You're familiar with the drawing room," she said, leading the way upstairs and into the most respectable room in the entire house, "but I'm afraid it's not spacious enough for dancing."

She pushed open the double doors into the adjoining chamber. There were several wooden chairs in a group by the fireplace, but apart from these, it was devoid of furniture. There were no pictures, no ornaments, and in a few places, the plaster had discoloured.

"This one is larger, which makes it more suitable, but as you can see, it's somewhat bare and shabby. Eugenia had grand plans to redecorate it, but I dissuaded her from putting them into action, as I suspected I could ill afford what she was suggesting."

To her relief, Peter gave a nod of approval. "The emptiness of this room isn't a problem. If anything, it's a blessing. Most people have to clear their furniture out in order to make space for dancing. All we need to do is to bring some more chairs in, to accommodate those guests who wish to sit and watch. We can hide the dreariness with greenery—"

"I don't think Eugenia would approve of that."

"But do you approve?"

"Yes."

"That's all that matters. It is your party, not hers. What about musicians? Have you hired any players yet?"

"No. I wasn't certain what I needed, and when Eugenia said she would arrange it, I feared she would spend too much on my behalf and told her not to bother."

"I know a few people who might be able to help. Leave that with me. Can you manage the food?"

"Yes. Susan and I have already discussed that. We're sure we can provide a supper to rival Eugenia's for a fraction of the cost if we prepare it all ourselves."

"Better, if the pie you fed me on the coach is anything to go by."

"You remember?"

"The flavour is impressed upon my taste buds forever."

"I made it."

"Did you? I thought Susan was the cook."

"She is, but I was her kitchen maid long before I rose to the exalted heights of waiting on Miss Whittaker."

"Then the memory has just become even more special to me."

"What about drink?"

"That's one expense I fear you'll have to bear. Your guests will expect wine, as well as lemonade and orgeat. I'll talk to Miss Lane. See if I can persuade her to prepare her Wassail Bowl for us."

"If not, we could try to concoct some, but it wouldn't rival the excellence of Miss Lane's."

"Don't waste time trying to perfect your recipe yet. I'm sure our friends will be happy to help."

"Do you honestly think so? Even when they discover I am nought but a servant who owns—at the moment, at least—a house?"

"I do. You concentrate on preparing the food, and leave the rest to me."

Meg had no choice but to do so. Whether she wished to or not, her ignorance and lack of funds forced her to depend on Peter's aid.

Despite everything, she found it was a relief to rely on him. He had broken her heart in two, but he had not deserted her.

And for some inexplicable reason, she still trusted him to rescue her.

Chapter 25

Peter left Meg's house, determined to prove he was still her friend, though he no longer had anything more to offer her.

It would be laughable—if it didn't hurt so much.

Meg had feared he'd be disgusted by her background, and to impress him, she'd plunged into expenditure she couldn't afford. Yet it was the illusion she'd created which had kept him from proposing marriage, fearing others would think him a fortune hunter!

What a fool he'd been to think she was above him. If only he hadn't held back, they could have faced this current crisis together. A crisis on two fronts—her need for money and his disgrace.

But it was too late for that. He couldn't propose to her now and force her to share his shame. It would make him worse than a fortune hunter, as he hadn't even a good name to offer her.

He hadn't intended to encourage Meg's aspirations to be a lady, but he held himself partly responsible. Motivated by duty and affection, he would help her save Mrs Frampton from embarrassment, however much he disliked the woman.

He could not blame Meg's friend for reminding him of the lady he'd rather forget.

Peter spent the rest of the day with Annie. Unable to face the thought of being inside, he took her for a walk around the harbour, as far away from Meg's house as possible.

"Am I to have a new mother?"

Peter's stomach clenched. How could he tell his daughter the truth? She was too young to understand.

"You didn't ask her, did you?" she said in a small voice.

"No. Miss Harding was upset."

"Why? What did you do to her?"

Though he knew he was to blame for adding to Meg's suffering, he concentrated on the initial cause of it. "She was distressed about her party. She's never organised one before, and she didn't realise how hard it would be, or how much it would cost."

Dear Annie. She didn't flinch an iota when she learned Meg was not so wealthy as she thought.

"Oh. Will she have to cancel it?"

"She doesn't want to, but she needs our help."

His daughter leapt at the challenge, and started to list the things Meg might require, as if she planned parties every day.

"Woah! You don't need to organise the entire event. I hoped you could persuade Miss Lane to prepare her famous Wassail Bowl for her."

Annie shot him a smug smile. "Consider it done."

"And maybe help to decorate her rooms?"

"I will see what I can do."

The conversation passed onto other things, and Peter needed to say little to keep his daughter chattering.

As the light faded, they returned to Miss Seymour's.

Outside the door of the school, Annie paused and laid a hand on his arm. "Don't worry, Papa. I'll look after your Miss Harding for you."

She kissed his cheek and tripped inside before he could deny she was his Miss Harding, and that, sadly, she was never likely to be.

After leaving his daughter, Peter strode toward Jethro's house. If he was going to help Meg make her party a success, he needed more than Annie's support.

Careful not to interrupt his friend's routine, Peter joined Jethro in the drawing room just before five as usual, a few moments before dinner was announced.

When they'd helped themselves to the dishes spread on the table, and the footman had withdrawn, Peter knew the moment had come. With a brief prayer that his words would fall on fertile ground, he broached the subject on his mind.

"I need your help, old friend."

"Do you indeed."

"It's about Miss Harding."

Jethro eyed him curiously. "I know nothing about women. What possible assistance could I give you? It can't be that hard to ask her to marry you. At least you have experience of such a thing. I have no notion how to go about it. Get someone else to help you. Not me."

Pain seared through Peter's chest. "I'm not going to propose to her."

His friend rested his knife and fork on his plate and stared at him. "I'm no expert on such matters, but I thought your feelings were seriously engaged."

"They were—they still are, if you must know. But things have changed—for both of us."

Jethro waved a hand, encouraging Peter to continue, and resumed eating his dinner.

"Miss Harding is—was—a servant. Miss Whittaker's maid, not her companion, as everyone believed, including myself."

Jethro paused with his fork in the air and flared his nostrils. "If she lied to you, you are well rid of her."

"She didn't lie to me. The fault was mine. I assumed, and when she tried to correct my assumption, I misunderstood what she was saying. Her only mistake was aspiring to be what she wasn't—a lady. She had learned enough from her mistress to pass herself off in society, but though she inherited a house and a small amount of capital, no one taught her how to make her expenditure meet her income. As a result, she's run up accounts all over town, and will be forced to sell her home in order to pay her debts."

"Why are you set on defending her? She's acted foolishly, and deserves to reap the consequences."

"Because I love her. Though I don't expect *you* to understand that."

"Then marry the foolish woman and—"

Peter pushed back his chair and rose from the table. "I won't stay and listen to you malign Meg. She made a mistake and desperately needs our support, and I'm just as much a fool as her, because *foolishly,* I came to my best friend, thinking he would help me—"

"Sit down, Crowley," Jethro said. "You know my tongue sometimes gets the better of me. Of course you can depend on me. But if you're so besotted that you'd fall out with me over her, why in heaven's name won't you marry the girl?"

Peter slumped back down into his chair. "Because I can't."

"Why not?"

Deep frustration swept up Peter's body and came out in a heavy sigh. "I've been dismissed."

Jethro huffed. "I warned you how it would be with Lord Barnes. A testy fellow if ever there was. You'll get another role, one more suited to you."

"That's just it. I'm not sure I will." Peter dipped his eyes to his plate, though the food no longer appealed, as it turned to sawdust in his mouth.

"Go on."

"I didn't leave Mr Elsworth's of my own volition. I was dismissed. There was a scandal involving a lady's reputation. I promise you I was innocent, but I bore the blame."

The heat shot up his neck and flooded his face as he let his words sink in, wondering whether he had lost his friend's good opinion forever.

"Your word against hers, I take it?"

Peter nodded, feeling as helpless now as he had done at the time.

"I don't need to know why the lady would make such an accusation, but if you say you're not guilty, I believe you."

A weight fell off Peter's shoulders. He hadn't realised how important it was to him that Jethro still had faith in his honesty and his innocence.

"Thank you. That means a lot to me. Mr Elsworth felt just enough doubt about what happened to give me a brief reference. This satisfied Lord Barnes, but as chance would have it, he met my previous employer and his wife over Christmas and the truth about my dismissal slipped out."

"And yet you request my help for Miss Harding, and not for yourself?"

"Is it so surprising? My keenest desire is to lessen her distress, if I can. I've let her down badly."

"What do you want me to do for her?"

"Her most pressing problem is the entertainment she's supposed to be giving on Twelfth Night. Meg has little money left, but she's desperate not to let her new friends down. If you lent her some furniture, and a few servants for the day, and graced the party with your presence—"

"What? Why do you need me to attend? You know events like that make me squirm."

"First, it would do you good."

"Pshaw!"

"Second, and I'm certain this will sway you, I have a profound feeling we might require your support."

Jethro sniffed hard. "Very well. I'll come, though what assistance you think your socially inept friend can be, I shudder to think."

"Don't put yourself down. You're a very eligible bachelor. The ladies will be mad for you—"

"I doubt it. All I have to do is scowl, and they run a mile."

"Then don't scowl."

They finished their dinner in silence, but after the covers were cleared, Jethro didn't return to his desk, leaving Peter to enjoy his glass of port alone, as was his habit. Instead, he sat with him, deep in thought, though still not drinking, as he never touched spirits.

At length, Jethro spoke. "I wish to make you an offer, but I hesitate for fear of offending you."

Peter gave a bark of laughter. "I am way past being offended, my friend, and am grateful for any help you can give me."

"It's only a humble role, and considerably below what you're used to, but I could do with an extra pair of hands at the warehouse. If I impress upon you how greatly it would assist me—"

Jethro broke off, staring at his face as if trying to gauge his reaction to his suggestion.

Inside his mind, Peter tussled with his pride. Had he fallen so far that he—a gentleman's son—should be grateful for the offer of a position as a warehouse lackey?

Yes, he had. His gratitude defeated his pride with one swipe. "Thank you. I'll take it."

"I insist you stay here with me until your circumstances improve."

"Again, I'm grateful, but there's Annie to think of..."

His voice cracked. Meg wasn't the only person he'd failed. What would become of his daughter?

"I'll pay you a wage that will cover her school fees."

Peter sighed from the heart. "I don't know how to thank you. That's a tremendous relief. But I can't keep living here at your expense indefinitely, and how I'm ever to improve my circumstances—"

"Stop! It's not like you to have such a gloomy outlook, and it doesn't suit you. Don't worry about tomorrow. Put your future into God's hands, and deal with today. Leave tomorrow to worry about itself. Each day has more than enough worries of its own."

Peter knew he was right. He had to trust that God was still in control of his life, even if it didn't feel like it.

He had so much to be grateful for—a friend who believed in him, a roof over his head, and work for tomorrow.

And he had not lost Meg's friendship, though he yearned for more.

In this, at least, he hoped he would not let her down.

Chapter 26

Next morning, Meg joined Susan in the kitchen before the sun was up. Somehow, she'd convinced her that the party must go ahead.

Her capable friend had produced a detailed list of all the dishes they needed to provide for the supper, and what ingredients were required.

"I've bought most of these items already, but we'll leave the meat until the end of the week to ensure it's fresh for the party. The cakes will keep, so let's start with those. I'll prepare the plums while you make the raisin buns."

Meg had just put the first batch of buns in the oven when John appeared at the door, an uncertain expression on his face.

"What's the matter?" she asked.

"Visitors. What shall I do with them? Show them down here?"

"Heavens, no," Meg said, shuddering at the thought of Eugenia finding her up to her arms in baking. "Tell them I'm not at home."

John looked confused. "But you are."

"It's a polite way of saying you don't want to see anyone."

"The young'un will be disappointed."

She jerked her head up at his words. "Who do you mean is here, John?"

"Me," cried Annie, pushing open the door. "Please don't turn us away when we're here to help you."

There was a catch in Meg's voice as she asked, "We? Is your father with you?"

"No. He had to work, but I've brought Miss Seymour to lend a hand."

"She's come to help *me*?"

"Papa said you needed our support, so here we are. May I bring her down?"

The thought of the elegant headteacher in her kitchen made her tremble, stretching her imagination to the limit. But if she was kind enough to offer her assistance, Meg would humble herself to accept it.

She nodded, earning a satisfied grin from Annie, who scurried out the door, returning a few minutes later with Miss Seymour.

"I heard from a little bird"—the teacher tilted her head toward Peter's daughter with a half-smile on her lips—"that organising your Twelfth Night party was proving rather more tricky than you'd anticipated. Is that true? Because I have no wish to offend, if my information is faulty."

Meg wiped her floury hands on her apron and took a deep breath. "The truth of the matter is, I've no experience and no money."

In as few words as possible, she explained her circumstances and waited for her visitor to leave in disgust, but Miss Seymour just shook her head, a look of amazement on her face.

"I do not know how you did it, Miss Harding. To maintain the appearance of a lady whilst running a place this size with only the three of you is nothing short of incredible."

"You don't blame me?"

"For what? Wishing to better yourself? Absolutely not."

"For hiding that I was a servant before inheriting this house."

"Resist the urge to chastise yourself for not advertising your true position in Miss Whittaker's household. Most of us have things in our past we'd rather hide. All kinds of mischief can result if people form assumptions and don't bother to find out if there's any truth in them. It is not a crime to keep a secret, Miss Harding. Tell me how I can help you."

"I need to make my rooms presentable. Mr Crowley had a few ideas—"

"Which he shared with us. We can bring over the greenery from the schoolroom to decorate, if you're satisfied with that suggestion. I checked this morning, and it's still fresh enough."

For a moment, Meg hesitated, recalling how Eugenia had scorned the notion when it had been proposed before. But then Peter's words came to mind, and she realised his opinion was far more important to her than Mrs Frampton's.

Her sophisticated friend would doubtless disapprove, but this was her party, and as this was a way of dressing her rooms without cost, she welcomed it with open arms.

"That would be wonderful. Thank you."

"Good. Joe will help bring it over on Friday. What are you planning to serve for supper?"

Meg introduced her to Susan, who showed her the list she'd prepared. Miss Seymour studied it, nodding her approval, and made one additional suggestion, which was added to the bottom of the page.

"Later in the week, I'll bring Sarah with me, to concoct her Wassail Bowl that Mr Crowley likes so much, but for today, what would you have me do? You need not be afraid of putting me to work. It won't be the first time I've prepared food, and I'm sure it will not be the last."

Taking the woman at her word, Meg set her the task of chopping vegetables for the soup, whilst Annie helped her make a second batch of buns.

Her spirits felt lighter than they had in a while, but she couldn't squash the disappointment that Peter had rallied his friends to help her, rather than coming himself.

He'd told his daughter he needed to work, but what did he mean by that? She knew he was no longer employed by Lord Barnes.

The conclusion she reached was not a cheerful one.

Though Peter had offered his friendship, he meant to increase the distance between them.

Chapter 27

The day before the party, Meg was already hard at work making bread when Annie ran into the kitchen.

"We've brought all the greenery from the school, and some other bits Miss Seymour thought might brighten up your rooms. Do you want to come and see?"

"I can't right now, Annie. I'm half-way through kneading this batch of dough, but ask John and he'll help empty the cart."

"Oh, there's no need for that. He and Joe have already carried everything into the drawing room. Shall we go ahead and decorate? It's a shame Papa had to work today as well, but I'm sure we can manage without him. If you ask me," she added in a whisper, "I think Miss Day is itching to try her hand at arranging the greenery, so if you just give the word..."

Meg pressed her lips hard together, trying to push past her disappointment that Peter had stayed away again, and listen to what his daughter was saying. She had not realised how forbidding her expression was until the girl addressed her once more, in a troubled voice.

"We can wait for you, if you'd prefer. Or come and help you chop vegetables. Or—"

"Run along, Annie, and get started," said Miss Seymour, walking into the kitchen in time to hear her last words. "Miss Harding can carry out any adjustments she wants later."

Meg watched as the girl skipped out of the room.

"I hope you don't mind me encouraging them to begin. Annie's warm-hearted, if over enthusiastic at times," the teacher said, her eyes twinkling, "and you seem somewhat distracted."

Unwilling to admit that Peter was occupying too many of her thoughts, Meg hastened to provide an alternative reason for her lapse in concentration. "I confess I'm feeling overwhelmed—with all that still needs to be done, but also with your generosity in coming to give me a hand."

"It is a pleasure, Meg, to support a friend. To ask for help is to take a risk, and you can only ask that of those you trust. I am honoured you trusted me with the truth, and hope you'll forgive me for sharing your story with your other friends at the school. We all want to help."

Meg's heart warmed at her words. It was a comfort not to be in this alone.

"Sarah has promised to mix her Wassail Bowl, so if you show her where she can work, she'll get started. The children will be safe with Miss Day. They'll mind what she says, and Annie has a good eye, so you needn't fear the decorating will have to be redone after they've finished."

"As I have no notion how to decorate a room for a ball, I'm delighted to let them do it for me."

"I suspected as much. Now, what would you like me to do?"

Susan, who'd been working in the corner of the kitchen, preparing some meat for the oven, directed Miss Seymour to an enormous pile of fruit destined for tarts.

As they chopped, and kneaded, and mixed, they fell into comfortable conversation, and time flew by.

When the decorating was finished, Annie begged them to step upstairs.

The result was everything Meg could have hoped for. The rooms had been transformed, their shabbiness hidden by the greenery which adorned every mantelpiece, beam and doorframe. Pictures hung on the walls, which had been starkly empty, and even the evergreen tree had found a place on a table at one end of the drawing room.

The winter light was fading when Susan called a halt to the proceedings and invited them all to sample the cake she'd just taken out of the oven. Meg poured the tea and gazed around the kitchen at those who had worked hard at her side all day.

She thanked God for this caring group who'd shown her such kindness since coming to Weymouth. Real friends who didn't require her to be something she wasn't.

Was that the sign of a true friend? Someone who accepted you for who you were, and loved you regardless? Someone you felt comfortable accepting help from. People you trusted with your secrets.

Would her relationship with Peter have worked out any differently if she'd treated him as a true friend, and shared the truth about her past with him from the start?

Perhaps if she'd trusted him fully, they could still be friends. She'd thought that was what he'd offered her, but what was she to think now, when he seemed to be avoiding her?

"Papa!" shouted Annie, bouncing up from her place on the bench, almost knocking her tea flying. She ran to embrace her father, who stood in the kitchen doorway.

Meg tried not to let herself be affected, but it was no use. Her heart leapt for joy just to see his beloved face again.

"May I come in?" he asked, directing his gaze at her.

"Of course you can," Annie said, trying to drag her father into the room, but Peter kept his feet planted by the door.

Although her heart thrummed loudly in her chest, Meg hesitated. Should she ignore the fact that he had sent others to help, rather than coming himself? Or overlook Annie's seeming ignorance that he was out of work?

No. She would not. Friends helped each other to do what was right. It was wrong of him not to tell Annie the truth.

"I don't know about that, Mr Crowley. I daresay you're after a piece of cake, but what have you done to earn it? Everyone else here has been working hard all day. What can you say in your defence?"

He stared at the hat in his hands for a moment before raising his eyes to her face.

"That I would have come earlier if I could, but I was needed at the warehouse." He paused, and his gaze passed over each of his friends, until it rested on his daughter. "That's where I work now—for Mr Hunt."

"But I thought you worked for Lord Barnes," Annie said, voicing her surprise—a feeling which, to judge by the gaping mouths around the table, was shared by everyone else.

Except Meg. Her reaction was quite different. Not shock, but untainted delight. It didn't matter to her that the work was inferior to what he'd done before. It was good, honest employment, and it reassured her that Mr Hunt must still believe in his integrity.

But it was the realisation that Peter hadn't been avoiding her which sent warmth flooding through her body.

"I'm sorry, Annie. What I'm about to say may upset you, but I'd rather you heard it from me, before someone else sees fit to enlighten you. Lord Barnes dismissed me for the same reason Mr Elsworth did. He believed I was guilty of something I didn't do, and there was a scandal which was hushed up, and I was sworn to silence. But now his lordship has found out, and he's furious with me."

Meg took pride in Peter's speech. What a hard thing for him to admit to his daughter. To them all.

And the fact she already knew of his dismissal emphasised the intimacy between them—an intimacy she thought she'd lost.

Tears welled up in Annie's eyes. "But it's not fair if you didn't do it."

"I know, sweetheart, but Mr Elsworth refused to believe me, and so did Lord Barnes."

Meg could hardly breathe as Peter stared at his friends, a wary look on his face. Were they about to desert him?

Miss Seymour rose and extended her arm. "If you say you're innocent, that's good enough for me."

Peter grasped her hand and shook it. "Thank you."

The others nodded and murmured their support, showing that the headteacher was not alone in accepting his word. They all believed he was telling the truth—because they trusted him.

The wariness disappeared, and the twinkle returned to Peter's eyes.

"Now, about that piece of cake..."

Chapter 28

Peter's spirits lifted to see his friends from the school rallying round to support Meg—coming to her aid when he could not.

He saw the intensity in her eyes as she teased him to justify his absence. Though he revelled in the knowledge she'd missed him, he knew it would be better for the welfare of his heart if he squashed such feelings.

It hadn't been his intention to announce his change in circumstances in such a public manner, but she'd gently forced his hand with her teasing and now it was done, he could not be sorry. His friends had accepted his word that he was innocent, and that consoled him somewhat for his inability to prove it to others.

Meg begged him to take a seat, poured him a cup of tea, and passed him an enormous wedge of cake.

He took a mouthful, savouring the heavenly taste.

"Just as well you gave in," he said to her, "otherwise who knows what might have happened. After all, I have it on good authority that men would kill for a bite of your pie."

Meg's lips twitched. "Much as I appreciate the compliment, I learned from the best, and the delectable recipes I make are only what she taught me. Susan prepared this cake—not me."

Peter complimented the other woman's cooking and ate a few more mouthfuls before he spoke again.

"I'm happy to accept my slice as a gift of friendship," he said with a grin, "but I hope you'll think I've earned it when I tell you I've secured us some musicians."

There was a general murmur of approval around the table.

"Mr Curtis is an excellent fiddler, and he has a couple of friends he's going to bring with him, whom he assures me will be happy to play in exchange for their supper."

"Then we'll have dancing after all," Meg said.

His daughter clapped her hands in glee. "It will be just like Christmas Day again. We've even put the mistletoe up for you—"

Peter's smile faded. It would *not* be like Christmas Day, when his hopes for the future had been very much alive.

The memory of kissing Meg that night was too precious to taint with a forced embrace in full view of her guests—people such as Mrs Frampton, who might despise the tradition of the mistletoe.

Or worse, find the notion too appealing and he definitely didn't want to be obliged to kiss *her*.

"I don't think that's a good idea."

Annie's face fell. She mumbled an apology and withdrew to the farthest corner of the kitchen, where Joe was playing with his toy soldiers.

Peter watched her go, disappointed to have upset her, before turning back to confront an equally crestfallen Meg.

Her doleful expression suggested she had misinterpreted his reaction to the mistletoe. Did she believe he was reluctant for another opportunity to embrace her? That he regretted kissing her in the semi-gloom of the schoolroom on Christmas Day?

No. That was a memory he cherished, and he had to make her understand.

"I don't think Mrs Frampton would approve. I suggest you take it down."

Meg's reply was non-committal, and he would have pushed the point, but he had no right to dictate to her. He could only hope she did as he suggested. Otherwise, there could be trouble, in more ways than one.

Miss Seymour seemed to sense the tension between them and redirected the conversation. "What do you intend to do once your party is over, Miss Harding? How do you plan to go on?"

"Not like I have been doing, that's for sure. I'm tired of pretending my past never happened, and besides, it's no longer an option. I've spent too much money, and we'll have to sell the house and move to somewhere smaller in order to have something to live on."

"What a shame! It's such a fine place. Is there nothing you could do to earn an income, to enable you to stay here? What are you good at?"

Meg shrugged. "Waiting on grumpy old ladies, and this." She waved her hand around the room. "The kitchen has always been a haven for me."

"Maybe you could set up a bakery," said Miss Day.

Susan shook her head. "Not here. It's a well-appointed kitchen, but you'd need big bread ovens to produce enough loaves and a shop from which to sell your goods. I doubt it would impress our neighbours if we erected a stall on the Esplanade outside our front door to market our wares, however tasty they were."

The women continued to talk through the possibilities, each plan discounted almost before it was suggested.

Peter was only half listening. He was playing with an idea that had popped into his mind. A way that Meg could stay here.

It was something Mr Curtis had said to him earlier, about acquiring a property for a client who wished to offer accommodation to seaside visitors. Why couldn't Meg and her friends do that?

"You could open a boarding house."

His voice cut through the hubbub, and everyone stared at him.

"Why not take in lodgers? The King might have ceased his visits, but Weymouth is still a popular sea bathing resort. Your location here on the seafront is ideal. You're near where the bathing machines are drawn up on the beach each day, and close to the assembly rooms kept by Mr Stacie. The libraries and shops are but a short walk away."

Meg furrowed her brow. "But we're just servants. You've seen what a mess I made of trying to be a lady. Do you truly think us capable of such an enterprise?"

"What is required beyond what you're already doing—cleaning and cooking? With a little help to manage your money, I see no reason you shouldn't succeed."

Meg rested one finger on her lower lip as she contemplated his suggestion. Her countenance lightened as the idea took root, but her eyes were still clouded with uncertainty.

He longed to reassure her.

"This gives you as good a chance as any of being able to stay here. If it's successful—and I'm certain it would be, with your genteel manner and Susan's delicious meals—you can hire servants, and might end up doing less housework than you do at the moment."

"Aha," Meg said, a wide grin spreading over her face. "Now you've got me. Looking after a cantankerous old woman was easy compared to keeping this place clean. Eugenia will never speak to me again, but I'm willing to give it a go. What do you say, Susan?"

"That you're forgetting the shabby state of this house. We'd need to decorate every single room, buy new furniture and bed-linen, and replace all the mattresses. It's impossible, as we don't even have enough money for fuel to get us through the winter."

"You could borrow the funds to finance the refurbishments," Peter said, "and repay it when you take in lodgers. There's some risk, I grant you, but you need not open the entire building at once. Earn some income and grow your business, one set of rooms at a time. If the enterprise fails—you can revert to your original plan to sell the house."

Meg shook her head. "I refuse to gamble with our future like that. What if there were no guests? We'd be in a worse position than we are now. No. After the party, I'll instruct Mr Curtis to locate a buyer for this house, and we'd better pray he'll find one quickly, or we'll have no option but to move to Cornwall and live with Susan's sister."

Peter forced a smile. He couldn't blame Meg for not wanting to get into any more debt.

"I understand—but it's a great pity you can't try it."

It was not until later that night, alone in his room at Jethro's house, that he was at liberty to examine his feelings. Why was he so bitterly disappointed Meg had discarded his plan to help her?

The truth hit him squarely in the stomach.

Even now, he harboured a hope—albeit a slim one—of a future with Meg.

He could offer nothing to entice her to stay at present, but his love burned as brightly as ever.

If his circumstances improved, and the dust settled on the scandal, he would ask her to marry him. He hoped she would overlook his tarnished past and say yes.

But if she sold the house, she might be forced to leave Weymouth.

And the thought of her going out of his life was too painful to contemplate.

Chapter 29

After her friends left, Meg sat in the drawing room alone, mulling over the events of the day and the emotions that had accompanied them.

It was a relief to discover Peter had not lied to Annie. Work *had* prevented him from coming to her aid earlier, and he'd cared enough to join them after labouring in Mr Hunt's warehouse since before dawn.

But though he had come, he hadn't lingered, and her old doubts crept back in when he departed with the others. She reasoned with herself he must be tired, but she missed having the chance for private conversation, and found it hard to convince herself he wasn't still pulling away from her.

She gazed for a long time at the mistletoe Annie had put up with such confidence. It was encouraging to know the girl's eagerness for her to marry her father had not diminished. If only Peter shared the same enthusiasm.

Would it be wrong to ignore his warning about the mistletoe? Was the memory of their kiss on Christmas Day so painful he had no wish to repeat it? Or did he regret kissing her at all?

Meg was no longer sure she understood the nature of the scandal from Peter's past. When he first told her, she'd assumed he'd compromised the reputation of a lady he felt honour-bound to offer for. But if her assumption was correct, why hadn't he married the woman already?

The more she thought about it, the less sense it made. Today, he talked of his innocence. What had he been accused of? And what was the price he had to pay? What scandal could be so great it scarred him for life?

Meg latched onto the most important fact. If he was not obliged to marry another woman, her hope for a future with Peter was not lost.

He'd upset her when he'd urged her to take down the mistletoe, but now she saw his warning in a different light.

Meg suspected he had some misguided notion of protecting her from the disgrace that had followed him to Weymouth.

Huh! She would put him right. She didn't want to be protected—she wanted to stand with him.

Meg would show him that, by making a little scandal of her own.

By forcing him to kiss her under the mistletoe in full view of her guests.

The following evening, Meg struggled to keep calm as she greeted her visitors. Would they approve of her arrangements, or would she be revealed for who she was in front of Eugenia and her elegant friends?

Mr Hunt had loaned her three servants for the day and sent over extra chairs and tables. He'd even deigned to grace the party with his presence, which, she learned, was a rare event.

Meg moved through the rooms, talking to her guests with a confidence she didn't feel, wishing Peter was at her side.

"What quaint decorations," she overheard one of Eugenia's friends say to another as she surveyed the room. "Fancy dressing your ballroom to appear like a wood."

Her companion agreed. "But ooh, do you see that tree, with all the candles lit? Who would have supposed it would look so pretty?"

Meg gripped her hands together to stop them from trembling as she interrupted their conversation. "I'm so glad you admire it. It's a German custom. Queen Charlotte has a candlelit evergreen at Christmas every year, so I've been told."

Both women looked impressed and moved away, bolstering Meg's confidence—until Mrs Frampton caught her eye.

She watched as Eugenia gazed up at the mistletoe, hanging over the double doors between the two rooms. How did she view the decorations?

Meg bit down on her lower lip as her friend's gaze lingered on the sight. Did Mrs Frampton consider her vulgar to have mistletoe in her ballroom? On reflection, it was more suited to the servants' hall.

But no. Eugenia's mouth turned up at the edges. That must be a sign of her approbation, and the tension in Meg's shoulders vanished.

At her request, Mr Curtis and his friends struck up a tune, ready for the dancing to begin. Miss Seymour informed her she should give the honour of calling the first dance to her most important guest, so naturally Meg asked Eugenia.

She regretted the impulse when she saw who Mrs Frampton had claimed as her partner—Peter.

All her enthusiasm for taking part melted away, and she left the ballroom on the excuse that she must check the supper room was ready, to avoid partnering anyone else.

As the music drew to a close, Meg re-entered the room, hoping to secure Peter's hand for the next set.

Her progress was halted by a guest who complimented her on the success of the evening.

While it was gratifying to know they were enjoying themselves, it delayed her progress so much that once more, she had to witness Peter standing up with another acquaintance.

Meg resolved to ensure he had a better chance of claiming her hand for the opening dance after supper, but meanwhile she spied Annie sitting on one side of the room, swinging her feet under her chair, as she watched the set forming.

"Would you care to dance the next with me, Miss Harding?" asked the curate, who had approached while she was distracted.

She was about to accept when a thought occurred to her. "Would you mind, very much, if I offered you a different partner, Mr Barnes? I have a young friend sat over there"—she nodded toward Peter's daughter—"who, if I'm not mistaken, is desperate to join in."

"Has her father given his permission?" he asked.

"He has."

"Then I'll see if she will stand up with a gentleman twice her age."

Meg chuckled to herself as Annie jumped up from her chair and placed her hand on Mr Barnes's arm. That was a job well done.

It was over an hour later that her guests trickled out of the supper room, praising the vast array of dishes. She must be sure to pass onto Susan the many compliments she'd received on the quality of the fare.

Relieved that the evening was a success, Meg relaxed and decided to rest her legs before the dancing resumed. She found a quiet seat in the corner of the drawing room, near the candlelit tree, and hoped Peter would find her there.

After a short while, a man sat down beside her. It was not Annie's father, but Mr Curtis, taking a well-earned break from playing his fiddle.

"Thank you for coming to my aid tonight," she said. "Your talent on the violin is to be envied."

The solicitor bowed his head. "It's been a pleasure. I'd play for my supper every evening if I could guarantee such excellent food."

Meg accepted the compliment with a smile, but it faded almost at once, as she realised she should take this opportunity to ask him about selling the house.

Before she could speak, Mr Curtis spoke again. "I have a proposal for you, Miss Harding."

Her mouth dropped open in surprise. Heavens! How unexpected.

When she jerked her eyes round to his face, she saw he was chuckling.

"Forgive me. Not *that* kind of proposal. Crowley informed me you were having some financial difficulties, and might be forced to sell your house."

Heat rushed to Meg's cheeks. Had Peter told everyone of her problems?

"He also mentioned his suggestion that you should open a boarding house, and why you'd abandoned the idea. My needs are simple. I spend much of my time in my office, and need little in terms of furniture apart from a comfortable bed to sleep on, but I do enjoy a well-cooked meal, and my current lodgings are proving far from satisfactory. To put it mildly, I'm becoming desperate. Would you consider letting me rent a suite of rooms in your home and providing me and my valet with breakfast and dinner every day?"

Meg bit her lip. If only it were possible.

"I'm sorry to disoblige you, really I am, but I fear my circumstances are so straightened that I couldn't even engage to provide you with a comfortable bed."

"I thought that might be your answer. What if I paid for six months' board and lodging in advance?"

"Six months?" Meg said in a voice full of wonder.

He nodded. "I see I've taken you by surprise. I won't push you now, but please think about my offer, and pity me. If I have to tolerate Mrs Simm's cooking for much longer, I'm going to be all skin and bone."

Without giving her a chance to reply, Mr Curtis bowed and moved back to the ballroom, ready to pick up his fiddle again.

Meg rose from her chair, her head in a spin. Perhaps the idea of opening a boarding house wasn't so impossible after all. She must find Peter to discuss the matter with him.

But when he came up behind her, a few moments later, all thought of taking in lodgers fled from Meg's mind.

"May I claim your hand for the next?" he whispered in her ear. He stood so close that his breath warmed her neck, making her shiver delightfully.

"I should like that. It would be a shame not to dance at my own party."

But Meg didn't enjoy standing up with Peter as much as she should have done. The entire time, she was debating whether or not she should make him kiss her.

She wanted to feel his lips on hers again, and when the music ended, she steered him to where the mistletoe hung overhead and paused.

Even as she hesitated, she realised she could not do it. She couldn't force his embrace.

She dropped his arm as if it had become red hot. "Pray excuse me, I must see to the...um...lemonade."

Peter gave her a strange look as she hurried away, and she hadn't moved far before she turned back, determined to give him the chance to kiss her, if he wished.

To her horror, she found Eugenia had taken her place at Peter's side—under the mistletoe.

Chapter 30

Peter's breathing stumbled as Meg turned back toward him, her face clouded with uncertainty, and, he thought—hoped—regret.

Their eyes met, and it felt as if the two of them were caught in a moment of time, while the rest of the people in the room carried on in a blur of activity.

Why had she manoeuvred him under the mistletoe, and then deserted him? Had she feared he would reject her kiss?

The notion had not even crossed his mind, though the more responsible part of him said it should have. Despite his previous resolution, he had been only too ready to taste her lips again, and his heart still thrummed in anticipation of the kiss that had never come.

Because she'd left him standing there, rejected. Did she regret leaving him now?

While he watched, mesmerised, the colour drained from her face, shattering the moment as if it was made of glass. Alarm coursed through his body. Why did Meg look so ashen—so pained?

At the same instant, he felt a touch, and tensed as he saw Mrs Frampton stood next to him, curling her hand possessively around his arm.

"Why, Mr Crowley," she purred. "What a singular place to stand. Were you waiting for someone?"

Peter swallowed hard. He needed to get away from this woman. Fast. "If you'll excuse me, I'm parched. I need something to drink."

She did not release him. "Fie! You mustn't fly in the face of tradition. It would be such a shame if no one availed themselves of the opportunity to steal a kiss. There are plenty of berries, after all. Perhaps we should set an example."

His breathing became laboured. He had no intention of kissing Mrs Frampton or anyone—except Meg.

The longer she kept her grasp on his arm, the more his agitation grew. "I really need that drink. Would you care to accompany me to find a glass of lemonade?"

Peter tried to move her away from the doorway, where the mistletoe hung, but she stood her ground, refusing to submit. "Not yet." She glanced upward. "Come now, don't tell me you're shy?"

He calmed himself. This was not the same as before. They were not alone. This woman could not damage him as *she* had done.

But he could not stand here, letting her fawn over him, with Meg watching on. With his free hand, he unhooked her fingers from his arm.

A chilling male voice rang out across the room. "Unhand my wife!"

Everybody fell silent, staring at Mr Frampton, who had just entered through the other door.

And then all eyes switched to Peter.

His head spun. This could not be happening. Not again.

Mrs Frampton's hand, which moments before had clung to him, dropped to her side as if it had been burned. She ran to her husband and stared up into his face, a picture of innocence, as he put a protective arm around her.

Before Peter could react to Mr Frampton's accusation, Meg hurried across the room toward his accuser. She bobbed a demure curtsey, but there was nothing meek about her determined expression.

"I'm sure you mistake the matter. Mr Crowley was merely accompanying your wife to fetch a drink or—"

"It pains me to disillusion you, Miss Harding, but I know better. Do you realise what manner of man you are entertaining?"

"Guard your words, sir. Mr Crowley is my friend, and I'll not have you malign him under my roof."

Peter glowed with warmth at Meg's vehement speech in his defence, but dreaded what was about to come. What had Jethro's rival learned of him that had provoked such a direct attack?

Mr Frampton had the gall to sneer at her. "I won't be silent. This man has deluded us all. He has wormed his way into respectable households to take advantage of defenceless women as soon as their menfolk's heads are turned. I tell you he is a snake."

Peter felt Meg's gaze upon him, but he just stood there, unresponsive, as if made of rock, unable to do more than observe the proceedings.

"I'm sure you're mistaken," she said, but with less conviction than before.

"I am not. This man was dismissed from his previous position because his employer caught him trying to force his attentions on his wife."

A gasp went up around the room. Heads bent toward their neighbours. They wondered at the allegations in hushed voices. Their expressions showed Peter he already stood condemned.

Meg's brows contracted, her eyelashes flickering with uncertainty. The sight pained him more than the accusations or the hasty judgement of the crowd.

"Come, Eugenia. We're leaving," Mr Frampton said with a final sneer in his direction. He bowed and moved toward the door.

"Wait," Meg called after him, and he turned back. "We have not heard what Mr Crowley has to say. Will you not give him a chance to refute your accusation?"

The man huffed and shook his head, his expression a mixture of condescension and pity. "Tell her, Crowley. Am I speaking the truth? Were you dismissed by your previous employer after being found alone with his wife—in her bedroom?"

Peter's mouth went dry. Every person in the room stared at him, holding their breath to hear what he had to say. Meg's gaze was expectant, hopeful, waiting for him to contradict what Mr Frampton had said.

He shot her an urgent plea with his eyes, begging her to trust him. "Yes, but—"

Peter wasn't allowed to continue.

The silence was shattered. The exclaiming and chattering began. No one wanted to listen to his explanation. To let him justify himself.

The circumstances had been damning, and they judged him guilty.

But he barely registered their reactions, as his gaze didn't waver from Meg's face. She raised a hand to cover her gaping mouth, but it did not shield him from the tortured look in her eyes.

Peter reflected on his promise to Mr Elsworth to say nothing about what had happened. He had kept his word—concealing the truth, even from Meg—but now the horror of that day had returned to haunt him.

At least he suffered no qualms of conscience that it was his fault the old scandal had been brought to light. What could have induced his employer to change his decision to keep the details of that dreadful afternoon between themselves, unless... Mrs Elsworth.

In his mind's eye, he was confronted with the image of her face, contorted by rage. She must be responsible for this.

Not content with tainting her husband's opinion of Peter's integrity, she had seen an opportunity to further her revenge, and she'd taken it, destroying his life here, too.

He wanted to scream his innocence, to convince Meg he was not guilty of misconduct, but the circumstances were damning. Would she even listen? Would it matter what he said in his defence if she no longer trusted him?

A sharp pain seared through his chest, depriving him of breath.

What he'd told her before had not been enough. He should have shared everything with her, despite his word to Mr Elsworth.

Faced with the stark truth about his dismissal, Meg had given up on him.

Peter bowed toward her, his anguish making his response sound harsher than intended.

"Please forgive me for causing a disturbance at your party. I will remove my contaminating presence at once."

Without giving her a chance to reply, he headed for the door.

Chapter 31

As Peter walked away from her, Meg shook so violently, she thought she was going to be sick. The shock of Mr Frampton's revelation rocked the very core of her trust in the man she loved. Did she know him at all?

She had accepted his explanation, that he'd lost his previous position because of a scandal over a lady, but she had not expected this. To have trifled with a married woman, the wife of his employer? It revolted her. How could he throw his Christian principles to the wind because his passions were too strong?

It was so out of character for her Peter. It was... unthinkable.

Her breath caught at the thought. It *was* unthinkable. Beyond belief.

He had assured her of his innocence. Why would she stop trusting him, just because the scandal was more hideous than she had imagined?

A bud of hope formed in her heart. She must force him to speak up. If he wasn't guilty, there had to be something he could say to vindicate himself. To prove his innocence to them—and to her.

Peter was already at the door. A moment more, and he'd be gone.

If he left now, with these allegations hanging over his head, he could never show his face in Weymouth society again.

Meg had to act right away.

"Have you nothing to argue in your defence, Mr Crowley?" she asked in a loud voice, causing him to stop his retreat. "Are you guilty of what you are accused?"

Peter paused before pivoting on his heel and walking back into the room.

Nobody moved. Nobody spoke. Everyone was eager to hear the next instalment of the drama. It would probably keep Weymouth's gossips chattering for weeks.

His head, which had hung low as he retreated, now jerked upward, his gaze intense as it met hers.

The ghost of a smile crept onto his lips. "No, I am not."

A ripple of excitement spread through Meg's guests, but Mr Frampton sneered.

"Do entertain us with your explanations. I'm sure there is an excellent reason why Mr Elsworth found you with your arms around his wife, in a state of undress—what conclusion could he draw other than that you were trying to—"

"Enough. I'm innocent."

"Pshaw! Don't talk rot. How can you explain away such incriminating evidence?"

"Because *I* was there—and *you* were not."

Mr Frampton's colour deepened, but he kept his mouth closed.

"I was not forcing my attentions on Mrs Elsworth. You have my word on it."

"Huh! We're supposed to trust your word, rather than the lady's? Have you nothing more to offer in your defence?"

"What is the point? It's my testimony against hers, and if you won't accept my word, then you will not believe anything else I say. You must decide who is telling the truth. I can't convince you I'm blameless."

Meg watched Peter's confidence falter as he observed the sea of unkind faces surrounding him. Their expressions reflected their judgement, despite his cries of innocence.

Her lower lip trembled as she realised no one believed him.

His gaze met hers, his brow raised in question. They all thought he was guilty—but did she?

Uncertainty squirmed in Meg's stomach. She shut her eyes tight, unable to bear his piercing look.

She wanted to believe him—more than anything—but if the accusations were false, why wouldn't he defend himself? And why hadn't he revealed this to her before? Did he trust her so little?

No. It wasn't like that. He had confessed the scandal to her without prompting, but not shared the details, because he'd promised Mr Elsworth his silence.

And because she hadn't wanted to learn about this other woman, who had shattered her dreams of a future with Peter—the honourable, trustworthy man she loved.

The ends of her mouth curled up as Meg realised she still trusted him. If he said he was innocent, she believed him—whatever the accusation.

And her hopes of a life with him were not ruined, but very much alive—and she intended to grab them with both hands.

She opened her eyes, ready to give him her support, but to her dismay, she found she had hesitated too long.

Peter had gone.

Her faith in Peter restored, Meg desperately wanted to speak with him, but she couldn't chase after him until she'd informed her guests that one person in the room, at least, thought he was telling the truth.

"I believe Mr Crowley is innocent," she said, in a voice loud enough for everyone to hear.

Eugenia wrinkled her nose in disdain. "Do you dare to question my husband's words? Mr Crowley's behaviour was inexcusable and yet he tries to make out he's blameless. We must not be taken in by such ploys. He is beneath ladies like us, Margaret."

"He is my friend and I believe him."

"Didn't you hear what I said? The man cannot be trusted. If you refuse to follow my guidance on this, I will have no choice but to cut your acquaintance. It is him or me."

Meg chuckled to herself. Did Eugenia honestly think such an argument would sway her? "Him."

"I beg your pardon?"

"Him. I choose Peter."

Mrs Frampton's eyes flashed. "On first-name terms, are we? Then perhaps Mrs Elsworth is not the only woman he has seduced."

Anger welled up inside Meg until she thought she would burst. "How dare you talk to me like that? I may have been a servant most of my life, but my morals—"

"What did you say?" Eugenia squeaked.

Meg was almost betrayed into an ill-timed giggle at the outraged expression on the woman's face. What a pity Peter wasn't here to witness this.

She hadn't meant to advertise her origins, but the words had slipped out, and only as she spoke them did she realise she no longer felt ashamed of her past.

Despite her amusement at Eugenia's reaction, her anger had not abated. "Which part? About your rudeness, my Christian principles or that I used to be in service?"

"But you're Miss Whittaker's niece."

"No, I'm not. She sometimes thought I was, because she was confused, but I was only ever her lady's maid."

"Not her maid—her companion."

"Only because no one else could tolerate her bad-temper. We rubbed along together all right, and I stayed. Which is why she bequeathed me this place. It's been a fun few weeks, but now I've run out of blunt and," she said, recalling Mr Curtis's offer and prompted by a mischievous impulse to share the decision she'd reached, "I intend to open a boarding house."

The solicitor bowed his head toward her in acknowledgement, his wide smile showing his satisfaction at her words.

Eugenia's reaction could not have been more different. Her mouth worked, but no sound came out, so great was the shock of discovering her friend was not as respectable as she had supposed.

Mr Hunt made his way through the crowd to stand by Meg's side. "I, too, believe in Mr Crowley's integrity. I would trust him with my life. Moreover, I trust him with my reputation. What makes you think this tale is genuine, Frampton?"

The older man stuck his nose in the air, as if to answer his rival was beneath him. "Of course it's true. The lady told the story herself."

Meg had never seen Mr Hunt's face so expressive. He blinked and opened his eyes wide as his bottom jaw dropped. "She confided the details to you and gave you permission to make them public?"

Mr Frampton's cheeks coloured as his words floundered. "I...well..."

"No?"

"Lord Barnes laid no such prohibition on me—"

"Lord Barnes? Then you did not hear the story first-hand?"

"Are you doubting his lordship's word?" he asked, turning an even deeper shade of red.

"Not at all—but is it wise to place so much confidence in the lady's version of events? Does it not strike you as odd that she would spread such a tale that would make her the subject of gossip? I don't believe her husband would take kindly to you bandying his wife's name about in public."

Mr Hunt's masterful words affected Mr Frampton as powerfully as Meg could have wished. She thought the man looked like a trapped hare.

The curate came forward to join them and added his mite. "I also have faith in Mr Crowley's word and only wish my father's was more trustworthy. He should not have shared this story, Mr Frampton. I am witness to the fact that his lordship promised not to divulge what the lady had told him."

"Curtis, I may need your help," said Mr Hunt, calling across the room to the solicitor, who hastened to his side. "I would like my friend"—and he emphasised the word—"and employee, Mr Crowley, to be cleared of all blame."

"I'm sure it won't come to that," the solicitor assured him. "No one here would want to risk a case of slander. To believe stories heard second-hand, without attempting to verify the truth,"—he glared at Mr Frampton—"is folly enough. To repeat such a story, that condemns a man who claims he is innocent, is madness."

Mr Barnes nodded. "If you wish to establish the veracity of the tale, I suggest you ask Mr Elsworth. It is true he dismissed Mr Crowley, but he also provided him with a reference. A strange way to behave if he had lost faith in his employee. More like the act of a desperate man who wants to be rid of everything that reminds him of his wife's folly. I'm afraid my father has been swayed a little too much by Mrs Elsworth's confidences."

Mr Frampton's colour remained high, his expression so contorted that Meg feared he might suffer an apoplexy.

"There is no need to say more. I may have acted in haste. My apologies. Forgive me for breaking up your party, Miss Harding."

The Framptons swept out of the room, followed by the guests who had come with Eugenia. Others bid a hasty goodnight and departed in their wake.

Soon, the only people left were the musicians, and those whom Meg counted as her friends.

"Another dance!" cried Annie, unperturbed by the drama of the evening.

The girl grabbed her hand, but Meg shook her head, a wry expression on her face. She was no longer in the mood for dancing. Not without Peter.

Would he come back when he saw the other guests leaving?

She doubted it. He probably thought he wasn't wanted.

Meg blinked her eyes several times to keep the tears at bay. She needed to go after him and tell him how wrong he was.

Annie stared at her, tilting her head to one side, as she shot her a lopsided grin. "I expect he's on the beach."

Meg needed no more encouragement.

Leaving the others to continue the party without her, she walked out into the cold in search of Peter.

Chapter 32

Peter strode out of the house without looking back. For a few moments, he stood there, lost in the dark, as his eyes adjusted to the gloom of the wintry moonlight. Then he crossed the Esplanade and walked down the beach until he reached the water's edge.

He picked up a pebble and catapulted it into the sea. Then he found a larger one to throw, which landed amongst the waves with a satisfying splash. Stone after stone he tossed into the bay, trying to find some relief from the pain inside.

When his strength expired, he collapsed onto the sand on his knees and cried out to God.

"Why, Lord? Is this the reward for righteousness—for rejecting Mrs Elsworth's adulterous advances? To make the woman so bitter, she would go to such lengths to take her revenge on me—and her revenge has been complete. What a shame she wasn't there to witness my humiliation. To see my heart being crushed in full view of everyone. I hoped Meg would not..."

"What did you hope?"

Peter jumped to his feet and rounded on Meg. "How long have you been there?"

"Long enough."

Her words were the last straw. Why had she come? To gloat? He felt his defences had been stripped bare and his innermost feelings put on display, without his permission. "Satisfied to know you've broken my heart? Go back to the house. It will do you no good to be seen with me."

She didn't move. "What do you hope?"

Peter could not bring himself to reply. To admit he had hoped Meg would trust him. Because she loved him.

But if she had cared for him at all, it can't have run deep, because this confrontation had not shaken her faith in him. It had shattered it.

He glared at her and strode away along the sand, just avoiding getting his feet wet in the waves.

"Do you want to know what I hope?" Meg asked, coming up behind him and grasping his arm so he had to stop.

Peter's whole body tingled under her touch, and he let out an exasperated sigh. Of course, he wanted to know what she hoped, and he would be a liar if he pretended he was not tempted to take her in his arms and forget she didn't trust him. That she believed he would trifle with another man's wife.

"You won't ask, but I'll tell you, anyway. I hope you'll forgive me for taking a few moments too long to come to my senses. Mr Frampton's accusation shocked me. It was so unexpected. When you said there'd been a scandal involving a lady and there were consequences, I thought you meant you were honour-bound to marry someone else. But there was nothing honourable in an illicit relationship. Which is when I realised it couldn't be true. I could not imagine my Peter being guilty of such disgraceful behaviour."

A flicker of hope sprung up inside him. "Then you believe me?"

Meg nodded. "I'm sorry I ignored your advice to take the mistletoe down. If I had known the trouble it would cause..."

"Why did you leave me standing under it?"

She bowed her head, mumbling her words, so he only just caught them. "Because I wished you to kiss me of your own free will, not because I'd forced you."

He pulled her into his arms. "What makes you think I didn't want to?"

She tilted her face upward. "Did you?"

Peter felt his self-control crumbling. She was close. So close. "Yes," he breathed.

"Then why don't you?"

"Because I cannot ask you to marry me."

Meg whimpered and broke free of his hold, putting some distance between them. He didn't try to stop her.

"Tell me you don't love me, and I'll leave."

He heard the hurt in her voice. Though it might have been wiser to keep his mouth shut, he couldn't.

"I can't. Because I do. I love you. It was agony to think you didn't trust me. That you thought me capable of—"

"But if you love me, why can't you marry me?"

"Because I have nothing to offer except myself."

"I accept."

"You don't understand. Even if the gossip about tonight dies down, I have no means of securing another steward's role. I could be stuck working in Jethro's warehouse for the rest of my life."

"And your point is?"

"I can't support you, Meg."

"I can provide for myself."

"How? Last I heard, you'd spent your inheritance."

"I intend to open a boarding house, as you suggested. Mr Curtis is so desperate to be my first lodger he's willing to pay for six months in advance."

Bittersweet delight flooded his being. Meg could stay in her home. Her future was secure.

But his was not. He doubted he'd ever recover from the blows he'd received tonight.

"I'm pleased for you, but it changes nothing. A man should be able to support his family—"

"Peter Crowley, if I hear one more excuse from you, I shall question whether you really love me. Why should we be kept apart because of your foolish male pride? When you're done trying to protect me from your disgrace and your inability to provide for me, perhaps you'll recall I said yes."

The last of his resistance melted away. What a woman! She offered him what he could not ask of her—and it would be churlish of him to refuse his heart's desire. Not that he wanted to.

His nose twitched with amusement. "Did I propose?"

"Well, if you didn't, it's high time you did."

"Are you sure you want to marry a lowly warehouse worker with a shady background?"

"Was that a proposal?"

He smirked. "Meg, my darling, will you marry me?"

"I will."

"May I kiss you now?"

"Yes."

Peter slipped his arm around her back and drew her close. Resting his other hand on the side of her face, caressing her cheek with his thumb, he leaned in to claim her mouth with his own.

Chapter 33

As Peter's lips met hers, Meg's world stood still. The tide ebbed and flowed at their feet, but the only thing she was aware of was him—the strength of his arm around her waist, holding her tight, and the sweetness of his embrace.

Though the cold nipped at her fingers through her gloves, Meg didn't want this moment to end, but a gust of wind caught her unawares, making her shiver in Peter's arms.

He broke off his kiss, but did not relax his hold.

"What a beast I am, to keep you out in this biting wind, because I couldn't wait any longer to kiss you."

"You mistake the matter. It was beastly of you to need so long to be convinced to ask me to marry you—not for kissing me. You may take as long as you like for that."

"Is that so?" he asked, leaning in so close she could feel his breath on her face.

She closed her eyes in anticipation, but jerked them open again when she heard voices.

"There you are!" cried Annie, hurrying down the beach toward them, with Mr Curtis right behind her.

Meg stepped away from Peter, and he emitted a low growl at the interruption, making him sound like the beast he'd claimed to be a few moments before. It was rare for him to show any sign of annoyance, and she found the noise rather endearing.

"Annie, my dear. What brings you out here? Did you think we'd forgotten how to get back to the house?" Peter asked in a cheerful tone, which was so at odds with the feral noise he'd just made that Meg wanted to laugh. She pressed her lips together hard to restrain the chuckle lurking in her throat.

Poor Annie. She failed to grasp that her presence was so unwelcome.

"Sorry, Crowley. I couldn't dissuade your daughter from coming after you. She was worried by your prolonged absence and feared Miss Harding hadn't found you, but—ahem—I see she has."

The man's eyes twinkled in the moonlight as he spoke, and Meg suspected he'd seen enough to understand how matters stood between them. Perhaps he had even heard the frustrated growl.

Peter tucked Meg's arm in his own, and guided his daughter up the beach toward the house.

"Thank you for your concern, Annie, but you need not have fretted. You knew I wouldn't abandon you. But it's as well you've found us, because it's high time Miss Harding came inside. She forgot to pick up a cloak, and she might catch a chill if she stays out here much longer."

"I hope you both intend to come back with us. It's quite safe to return. The Framptons have gone."

"Gone?"

"Miss Harding and Mr Hunt spoke up for you, and the curate told everyone he thought his father had overstepped the mark. Fancy Mr Barnes saying that about his lordship, but he did, and as you can imagine, that put Mr Frampton in his place..."

Annie did not draw breath the entire walk back to the house, chattering about who said what, until she had given Peter a full account of what had happened after he'd left.

"I'm sorry you had to witness all that," he said to his daughter, as she took off her pelisse and handed it to Mr Hunt's footman, who was still on duty in the hall.

She shrugged. "I'm not a baby any more, Papa. I never doubted your innocence. She must be a silly woman. Anyone who saw you and Mama together would know you believed in the sanctity of marriage, and would never, ever, go after someone else's wife."

Mr Curtis ushered Annie into the ballroom, allowing the newly engaged couple a moment of privacy before they faced the others.

"I believe I feel a little sorry for Mrs Elsworth," Meg confessed.

Peter's mouth fell open in surprise. "Why? I assure you there's no need. She is an unprincipled woman who would break her marriage vows at the drop of a hat, and her husband deserves better."

"Don't get me wrong. I don't approve of her behaviour—quite the opposite. If she'd understood your character, she would have known you would never embark on an affair. But I sympathise with her a little—just a very little—for thinking your kindness meant something more. There was a time when I feared I'd made that mistake. That though *my* feelings were engaged, you were only being kind to me."

Her words brought a lopsided smile to his lips. "I wasn't. Your sense of humour, and the cheerful way you endured Miss Whittaker's bullying, attracted me from the first, as did your unruly red curls, which kept escaping from your bonnet. The more domineering your mistress became, the more I wanted to rescue you.

"The seeds of love were planted before we parted ways at the coaching inn, and if the old lady hadn't become ill and taken you away from me, I expect I would have proposed before leaving Weymouth. Maybe then, the incident with Mrs Elsworth would never have occurred..."

Meg put a finger over his lips to silence him. "Don't. Even though I was half in love with you back then, I could not have deserted Miss Whittaker. No one should be left to die alone."

"Forgive me," he said, kissing her fingers as he drew them away from his mouth. "I thought only of my own sufferings, and yet you would have put her needs above your own. What a remarkable woman you are."

She shrugged. "I told you before, I owed her a lot. Besides, if I hadn't stayed until her death, I would never have received my inheritance. So you may thank God things worked out like they did, or we would have nowhere to live."

"I do thank Him for bringing you back into my life, and now that you're mine," he said, leaning toward her, "I—"

Annie re-entered the hall, forcing Peter to pull away again. "Are you coming? Everyone's waiting for you."

This time, he didn't growl at his daughter's ill-timed interruption. Instead, he gazed at Meg with such intensity that warmth cascaded through her body, flushing her cheeks and banishing the remaining traces of cold.

Annie led the way into the ballroom, oblivious to the besotted looks passing between her father and Meg. "I found them," she announced, drawing all eyes toward her.

Susan stepped forward, her brows drawn together as she studied their faces. "Is all well?"

Without turning his head, Peter located Meg's hand and squeezed it. Never in all her twenty-seven years had she felt as loved and secure as she did at that moment. She had fended for herself for so long that his protectiveness brought a tear to her eye.

But this was a time for laughter, not crying. "Very well."

Peter pressed her hand again before addressing their friends. "Thank you for standing up for me this evening. When I promised Mr Elsworth my silence, I did not know what it would cost me.

"From what Annie told me, Mr Barnes, you assessed the situation accurately. My employer's wife lured me to her room on a false pretext and declared her feelings for me. The notion that I would reject her advances had not crossed her mind, and the result was not... pretty."

"And so she had her revenge on you," said Miss Seymour, pursing her lips in disapproval. "*Heaven has no rage like love to hatred turned, nor hell a fury like a woman scorned.*"

"Rather apt—unfortunately for me. I'm sorry for Mr Elsworth's sake that the truth is out—for those who choose to believe it—but for me, it is a tremendous relief."

There was a general murmur of approval, but Peter raised his palm to command an audience once more.

"There is one other thing I'd like to say before we dance again." The adoration in his face as he gazed down at Meg made her legs feel somewhat wobbly. "Miss Harding has done me the very great honour of agreeing to be my wife."

As everyone offered their congratulations, Annie ran forward and threw her arms around Meg.

"I knew it. His eyes smiled the first time he told me about you, and I realised at once you were the one. But after you left Weymouth, I feared you and Papa would never see each other again. I guess God had other plans."

"I guess He did," said Peter, enveloping them both in his embrace.

"Can I call you Mama now, or do I have to wait until you're married? Will I come to live here? What about..."

Annie continued to chatter until one of the fiddlers struck up a tune and Mr Curtis asked her to stand up with him.

Peter led Meg to the top of the set and—free from the restrictions of polite society—she danced only with him for the rest of the night, full of blissful expectation for the future.

As the clock on the mantelpiece chimed three, the dancing drew to a close, and Susan invited the remaining guests to have another bite to eat before they went home.

"If that includes your pies, I expect my betrothed will be first in line," Meg said.

"That it does," her friend replied, blushing at the compliment.

Despite her prediction, Peter did not lead the way into the supper room. Instead, he stayed at Meg's side until all the others had filed out.

"Seeing to the needs of my guests as if they were your own already?" she teased.

"No," he said, taking her arm and leading her in the opposite direction, toward the drawing room. "I'm afraid my motives are much less altruistic. In fact, they're rather selfish."

Pausing in the doorway between the two rooms, he put a finger under her chin and tilted it upward until she realised where they were. Under the mistletoe.

"I hope you do not intend to leave me standing this time."

"I won't force you to kiss me if you don't want—"

Her words were cut off as Peter's mouth pressed against hers, sweeping her into a demanding kiss that left them both a little breathless.

He reached up, plucked a single white berry from the foliage, and shot her such a boyish grin that he looked much younger than his years.

"Dangerous thing, mistletoe. Any man could claim a kiss from you, if they found you standing here, and although I'm not tyrannical by nature, I find myself quite unable to bear the thought of anyone else taking that liberty with you. Which leaves only one course of action open to me, unless I am to take it down now."

"Is that so, my love?"

"Yes," he said, kissing her again, before plucking a second white sphere. "I must use up all the berries myself."

Meg snaked her arms around his neck and drew him in for another kiss.

"I was hoping you'd say that."

Epilogue

Eager to claim his bride, Peter spoke to the curate before he left the party, and the following Sunday, Mr Barnes read the banns for the first time.

Three weeks later, on the last day of January, Peter and Meg were married in St Mary's Church, with all their friends around them.

After the ceremony, they walked along the Esplanade to Meg's house—their house, now, he supposed—where Susan had promised them a wedding breakfast fit for royalty.

The sea was calm, with the winter sun glistening on the water, reflecting the way his life felt today.

Annie came up behind them and slipped her arm into Meg's.

"May I talk to Mama?" she asked, challenging him with a pert look. "You can't have her all to yourself, just because you're married."

Peter would have liked to argue the point. He would very much like to have his wife all to himself. Now. But he could wait.

He knew his daughter needed time with her new mother. It was a huge change for them all.

"*Mama.* How odd it sounds," Meg said with a laugh. "This morning, I had not a single relative to my name, and now I have both husband and daughter. A complete family."

Annie came to such an abrupt halt that they were obliged to stop. "Oh no. You cannot mean that."

Meg shrugged at Peter, bewildered, but he just chuckled. "I think Annie is a bit put off by the word *complete*. Indeed," he said, brushing his bride's knuckles with his thumb, staring down at her with all the longing in his heart, "I hope, very much, God will allow it to grow."

He could not drag his gaze from his wife's face, her cheeks flushing pink under its intensity. Peter knew the moment she caught his meaning, as her eyes grew wide and twinkled with delight. The sight brought out his deep chuckle again.

"Oh, yes. I hope God will bless us with lots of children. Everyone should have brothers and sisters, if they possibly can."

They resumed their walk, but Meg seemed distracted, biting her bottom lip as though some thought had crossed her mind that bothered her.

"What is it, love?"

"I've no notion how to be a mother. My own was not an example I wish to follow."

"I'm sure you'll do just fine," he assured her. "You only have to be yourself. That is example enough."

Meg seemed satisfied with his answer and gave her attention to Annie until they arrived at the house.

Susan was true to her word, and after they'd eaten their fill, the bridal couple mingled with their guests, all keen to offer their congratulations.

"I noticed the Framptons didn't attend. Not forgiven you yet?" asked Jethro, striding up to Peter before anyone else could grab his attention.

"Mrs Frampton hasn't pardoned Meg for her plans to run a boarding house. I think she's embarrassed she was ever associated with either of us. Suits me. I can't stand the woman."

"When do you plan to open?"

"Mr Curtis is moving in next week."

"Will you continue working alongside your wife once you've finished making the place fit for guests?"

Peter wondered at Jethro's hesitant tone, at odds with his normal confidence. Did it matter to Jethro what he did now? He'd told him he could no longer work in the warehouse, as he needed to help Meg prepare the house. But after?

Everything had happened so fast, he'd not given it any thought.

"I don't know what I'll do, once the place is up and running. Apart from keeping the accounts, I'm not much use. Huh! I suppose I'll have to give a hand with the cleaning, if only to take some of the burden off Meg.

"I wish we could afford to hire a maid or two, but we won't be able to do that until we make a profit. If only I still merited the wages I earned when I worked for Mr Elsworth..."

His voice trailed off. After the debacle at the party, his name had been cleared to some extent, but it had not provided him with a reference, and without that, he couldn't get another steward's post.

It was the only consequence of his past he hadn't been able to shake off.

"Then you're not averse to a position away from the boarding house, if the pay was high enough?"

"No, but I'll not have you inflate my wages to keep me at your beck and call in the warehouse. It wouldn't be fair to your other workers."

"But that's exactly what I want, Crowley. You in my warehouse, at my beck and call. As my manager."

"Your manager?"

He nodded. "Curtis has been urging me to share some of the responsibility for the business for months, but the thought of letting go, of trusting a stranger, held me back. I should have thought of you sooner."

Jethro leaned closer and named a salary that made Peter's eyes bulge.

"Don't think I'm coddling you. I expect you to earn every penny. What do you say?"

"To what?" asked Meg, coming up beside her husband and taking possessive hold of his arm.

"Mr Hunt wants me to manage his warehouse. With the pay he's offering, we could afford Annie's school fees, and a housemaid or two. Maybe a footman, as well, and a potboy for the kitchen."

He held his breath, waiting for Meg's response.

A smile even bigger than the one she'd worn all morning spread across her face.

"How can we ever thank you enough, Mr Hunt? You've put the seal on what is already the most wonderful day of my life."

Eyes shining, she leaned forward and pressed a kiss on Jethro's cheek.

Peter roared with laughter at his friend's expression—one of shock mingled with confusion.

Jethro grunted and scowled at him.

"It's all very well for you to laugh, but you know social occasions make me feel awkward. I can never think what to say to people—especially women."

"We'll have to find him a wife, Meg. There are plenty of single ladies here to choose from. Who do you reckon is most likely to capture his fancy?"

She gave Peter's arm a playful tap. "Stop it! You're making your friend uncomfortable. Just because you adore me, you can't assume everyone is ready to fall in love."

"Don't worry yourself, Mrs Crowley. I'm inured to your husband's teasing. But you can be sure of one thing. If—and I repeat, if—I ever feel the need to marry, I will most certainly not let him have a hand in choosing my wife."

He bowed toward them. "Pray excuse me. Until my manager starts, my business requires my attention. Good day."

Meg walked across to the window and stared through it, to the sea beyond.

Peter stood behind her, slipping his arms about her waist and holding her close.

"Happy?"

"So happy I feel like I might burst, and yet—"

A crease marred his forehead as he bent his head close to hers. "What is it?"

"I'm afraid. Part of me is already waiting for it to end. Nothing good in my life has lasted, and I fear something will happen, and my world will come crumbling down again."

He hugged her even closer to him. "Life is like the sea. Sometimes peaceful—sometimes rough. We never know what lies ahead. But God has been my anchor through the storms of the last few years, and we must trust Him to bring our ship safely into harbour at the end of our days.

"None of us knows the time God has given us on this earth. I can't promise you a life without sadness, but I can promise to love you and cherish you. To walk alongside you, till death us do part. I meant each word I said in church, Meg. Only death will tear me away from your side. We must live each day we have together to the full, making it count."

She nodded, and the smile, which had briefly disappeared, settled on her lips once more.

"You're right, of course. We must pour our energy into living this day to the full, rather than waste it worrying about tomorrow, and the troubles it might bring. Today, I married the man who stole my heart away, and I intend to remain blissfully in love with him, for as long as we both shall live."

She tilted her face up to his, and Peter's heart swelled to see his love reflected in her eyes.

"I love you, Meg."

And he leaned down and claimed her lips with his own.

Did you like it?

I hope you enjoyed reading *Miss Harding's Hope*.
If you did, please consider leaving a rating and/or review on Amazon, BookBub or Goodreads, because this encourages me and helps other readers to find my stories.
Thank you.

Read how Jethro Hunt learns to love in *Miss Vincent's Vow* (coming 2024)

AUTHOR'S NOTE

I hope you've enjoyed reading Peter and Meg's story, set in my home town of Weymouth, Dorset, on the south coast of England.

The scandal surrounding Peter and Mrs Elsworth was inspired by the Biblical story of Joseph, who rebuffed the advances of Potiphar's wife and was thrown into jail.

Although a work of fiction, I've made the historical detail and language as accurate as possible, based on my research at the time of writing. The only exception of which I'm aware is the clergy of St Mary's Church—I've created my own characters rather than use the real historical persons, as the curate plays an important role in the *Women of Weymouth* series.

To find out more about the history behind the story, take a look at the glossary and historical notes included in this book or visit my research blog: RegencyHistory.net.

My thanks go to my friends and family for their ongoing encouragement through the ups and downs of an author's writing journey. Special thanks to my beta reader, Abigail Flynn, and my husband Andrew for his constant love and support, both as my number one fan and editor. My plots would have far more holes in them without his developmental insights.

If you enjoyed reading this Christmas romance, please leave a rating or review because it encourages me to keep writing and helps others to find it.

Glossary & historical notes

Assembly rooms: A venue for balls and other social gatherings. In 1810, the public rooms in Weymouth were situated on Gloucester Row on the seafront and run by Mr Stacie, who also owned a hotel. The Master of Ceremonies was Mr Rodber.

Bandbox: A lightweight box made of pasteboard or thin wood used to hold light articles of attire.

Banns: A public announcement in a parish church of a couple's intention to marry. The banns had to be read out loud on three Sundays in the parish church(es) of both bride and groom before the wedding. The ceremony had to take place in the parish church of either the bride or the groom. This was by far the commonest way of getting married, although it was possible to wed more quickly by common licence. Couples could also marry by special licence, but this was expensive and rare outside the aristocracy.

Baron: The lowest rank in the English peerage.

Blind man's buff: A children's game where one player is blindfolded and must capture one of the others and guess who they are. Also called hoodman blind. Included in Joseph Strutt's *Sports and Pastimes of the People of England from the Earliest Period* (1801).

Blunt: A colloquial expression for money. Included in Francis Grose's *A Dictionary of Buckish Slang, University Wit, and Pickpocket Eloquence* (1811).

Box pew: A church pew which was enclosed by walls and usually owned or rented by a family in the parish.

Calling a dance: At a ball, the top couple in the set called the dance—that is, they chose the tune and figures to be danced.

Cap—to set one's cap at: To set one's cap at someone meant trying to gain their affection. It often referred to a woman doing everything possible to obtain a marriage proposal from a particular gentleman.

Card: A visiting or calling card was a small rectangular piece of card inscribed with a person's name and often, but not always, with their address.

Chaise: A carriage, typically with a single seat for two people.

Chaperon: A female companion for an unmarried lady.

Charades: A word game where players chose a multi-syllabled word, eg moonlight, and composed a verse describing the different syllables of the word using enigmatic language for the other players to guess. This version dates back to the 1770s. A variant more similar to the modern game using miming had developed by the 1840s and was originally called dumb charades.

Charlotte, Queen: Queen Charlotte (née Princess Charlotte of Mecklenburg-Strelitz) (1744–1818) was the wife of George III. They married in 1761, just a few hours after meeting. The marriage was a happy one and produced fifteen children but was overshadowed by the King's mental illness in later years. She is credited with the introduction of Christmas trees to England.

Christmas celebrations: Christmas Day was a public holiday long before the Regency began, but many of the traditions we associate with the season were not yet established. Customs varied from place to place, and between different classes, with more traditions being maintained in the country than in large towns like London. All the Christmas traditions I've included could have been a part of the festivities in 1810. You can read more about a Regency Christmas on RegencyHistory.net.

Christmas tree: Having an evergreen tree in your house at Christmas was a Germanic tradition brought to England by Queen Charlotte. In 1800, she is recorded as having a large yew tree, decorated with candles and hung with fruit and sweetmeats in papers for her Christmas Day celebrations at Windsor. You can read more about Christmas trees on RegencyHistory.net.

Churchwarden: A person appointed to assist the parish priest with the day-to-day running of the church, including keeping order during services.

Cotillion: Also cotillon. A lively French dance for four couples standing in a square set.

Crambo: A game where one player gives a word, and another player has to find a word which rhymes with it. Included in Joseph Strutt's *Sports and Pastimes of the People of England from the Earliest Period* (1801).

Crown: One of the principal inns in Weymouth, situated in St Thomas Street.

Curate: An ordained clergyman who was hired to assist the parish priest or carry out the duties of a non-resident priest.

Devonshire Buildings: A run of Georgian townhouses near the harbour in Weymouth built c1810. They still stand opposite the Weymouth Pavilion today.

Dinnertime: Dinner was the chief meal of the day. During the Regency, people ate at different times, from as early as four to as late as nine o'clock. The time depended on many factors, such as class, whether you were in the town or the country, whether you had visitors, and how fashionable you were. You can read more about dinnertime on RegencyHistory.net.

Dowdy: *An awkward, ill-dressed, inelegant woman*. Samuel Johnson's *Dictionary of the English Language* (1785).

Dowling, Mr: Mr Dowling's Classical, Mathematical and Commercial School was situated in Devonshire Street, London. From an 1814 advertisement in the *Morning Post.*

Drawing room: Short for withdrawing room. Ladies retired to the drawing room after dinner, leaving the gentlemen at the table to imbibe stronger drinks, such as port. It was the sitting room where the gentry received visitors.

The **Esplanade**: A road running along Weymouth seafront. According to Feltham's *Guide to all the Watering and Sea-bathing Places* (1813): *As the Steyne is the fashionable promenade at Brighton, so the Esplanade is at Weymouth. It is about half a mile long, and thirty feet broad, from whence the company may descend to the sands, and walk with as much comfort as on a carpet, while the invigorating sea-breezes are playing round them.*

Fichu: A scarf or piece of cloth worn in the neckline of a dress.

Foundling: *A child found without any parent or owner*. Samuel Johnson's *Dictionary of the English Language* (1785).

George III: King George III (1738–1820) reigned 1760–1820. He suffered from periods of mental incapacity, which finally led to the appointment of his son, the future George IV, as Regent in February 1811. His condition is thought to have been caused by a hereditary disease called porphyria. After his first serious bout in 1788–9, the King came to Weymouth to recuperate, helping to make the town popular. He visited Weymouth nearly every year after this until 1805. A statute of the King was erected on the seafront in his honour in

1809, at the start of the fiftieth year of his reign. You can read more about George III in Weymouth on RegencyHistory.net

Golden Lion: One of the principal inns in Weymouth. Situated on St Mary Street, the daily accommodation coach left from here for Dorchester around half past ten and returned about three or four in the afternoon.

Greatcoat: Long, heavy overcoat worn over a gentleman's jacket.

Heaven has no rage…: *Heaven has no rage like love to hatred turned, nor hell a fury like a woman scorned.* This is a quote from William Congreve's play, *The Mourning Bride* (1697).

Introduction: An introduction was more than just getting to know someone's name. A gentleman would be presented to a lady by a third party—a chaperon or friend who could vouch for the gentleman being a desirable acquaintance for the lady. Until formally introduced, a lady and gentleman were not supposed to talk to each other.

Jack Robinson: Before one could say Jack Robinson was a phrase meaning a very short time. In use from 1785.

Mail coach: The post was carried between Weymouth and London by mail coach. These distinctive vehicles were black and maroon with red wheels and bore the royal coat of arms. Horses were changed regularly to maintain speed and the armed guard had a post horn to alert turnpike keepers of their approach so they could open the tollgate in readiness without the coach having to stop. This made travel by mail coach faster than by a regular stage coach, but it was also more expensive. There was also limited availability as the mail coach took a maximum of four inside passengers, though sometimes a further three could travel on the roof.

Milliner: A person—usually a woman—who makes or sells women's hats. Although millinery and dressmaking were separate trades, contemporary advertisements show that some establishments offered both.

Miss W: Readers familiar with Jane Austen's *Emma* will recognise the vulgarity of Mrs Elton, who refers to her husband as Mr E. Freeling writes in *The Pocket Book of Etiquette* (1837): *Most persons who mix in society which is not quite select, have occasionally had their ears crucified*

by hearing a female address her husband as "Mr A," or Mr any other letter which patronized his cognomen. This is most atrocious.

Mistletoe: This semi-parasitic, poisonous evergreen plant lives on the branches of other trees. It has small, oval leaves and waxy, white berries, which grow in clusters from October to May. The tradition of kissing under the mistletoe at Christmas goes back at least to 1780s, and Stephanoff's *Popular Pastimes* (1816) refers to the custom of plucking off a berry for every kiss. You can read more on RegencyHistory.net.

Orgeat: A refreshing drink made from barley or almonds and orange flower water.

Pelisse: A long fitted woman's coat.

Prayer book: The prayer book in use in 1810 was the *Book of Common Prayer* (1662). This contains the forms of services and ceremonies of the Church of England, including the Bible readings, prayers and other responses used in public worship.

Priest: A Church of England priest is an ordained clergyman who can perform all the required duties, including consecrating the bread and wine for communion.

Rector: When used to refer to a clergyman, rector means an ordained priest who holds a church living, with the right to all the parish tithes and fees. Rector can also refer to the patron of the living, who appoints a vicar to act as clergyman in the parish, in exchange for part of the income to which he's entitled (the lesser tithes).

Regency: The Regency period was the nine years from 1811 to 1820 when the Prince of Wales, the future George IV, ruled as Prince Regent during the last illness of his father, George III.

Reel: A lively country dance.

Reticule: A lady's purse or small bag designed to carry around personal items that used to be kept in a pocket. Pockets became impractical when dresses became more streamlined, and so a reticule acted like a portable pocket.

Sarcenet: *Fine, thin woven silk.* Samuel Johnson's *Dictionary of the English Language* (1785). Also sarsnet or sarsenet.

Set-down: A snub, often by a person of some importance to someone of inferior social standing.

Snapdragon: A raucous amusement, sometimes indulged in by young people at Christmas. A bowlful of brandy containing raisins was set on fire, and then the players had to pluck out the raisins and eat them as quickly as possible. It often led to burned hands and scalded mouths.

Spanish Coin: *Fair words and compliments.* Francis Grose's *A Dictionary of Buckish Slang, University Wit, and Pickpocket Eloquence* (1811).

Speculation: A noisy round game played with cards and fish or counters.

Spencer: A short-waisted woman's jacket that ended just under the bosom.

Squab: *A stuffed cushion.* Samuel Johnson's *Dictionary of the English Language* (1785).

Steward: *One who manages the affairs of another.* Samuel Johnson's *Dictionary of the English Language* (1785).

St Mary's Church: St Mary's Church is the parish church of Melcombe Regis—the part of the town of Weymouth on the beach side of the town bridge. It stands on St Mary Street (sometimes called St Mary's Street). I have tried to make all the details historically accurate, with one exception. I've replaced the clergy with characters of my own—Mr Vincent, the rector, and Mr Barnes, the curate. The actual rector was Thomas Wyndham, who held the living from 1809 to 1849. The church still exists, and my husband and I worship there. The current building opened in 1817, replacing the one which stood in 1810, which was not large enough for the size of the parish. The altar piece—the *Last Supper*, painted in 1721 by Sir James Thornhill, a local man famous for painting the cupola of St Paul's Cathedral—was retained in the new building and still adorns the back wall.

Sweetmeats: Items of confectionery; fruits preserved with sugar.

Tollgate: A turnpike gate which blocked the way to travellers to make them stop and pay the toll for the stretch of road they were using.

Topsy-turvy: *With the bottom upward.* Samuel Johnson's *Dictionary of the English Language* (1785).

Turnpike: A tollgate or a road with a tollgate. Turnpike Trusts were set up by Acts of Parliaments during the 18th and 19th centuries in order to improve the state of the roads. Trusts maintained individual stretches of road and had the right to levy tolls on road users to finance this. A turnpike gate blocked the way to travellers to make them stop and pay the toll for the stretch of road they were using.

Twelfth Night: 5 January—the twelfth day after Christmas and the eve of the Christian feast day of Epiphany.

Wassail Bowl: A bowl of spiced wine or ale, which was shared at Christmastide. Also Wassel Bowl or Wassel Cup. According to Brand's *Observations of Popular Antiquities* (1813) it was traditionally carried from door to door by young women on New Year's Eve and accompanied by verses. The recipe I've used comes from an article in *The Examiner* (1817) which encouraged the revival of Christmas traditions. A response to the article stated that the Wassail Bowl was still a custom in some parts of the country.

Wessex, Duchess of: The Duchess of Wessex is a fictional character from my *The Merry Romances* series, who first appears in *A Perfect Match*.

Weymouth: A fashionable seaside resort in Dorset on the south coast of England, which rose to importance through the repeated visits of King George III. Its sheltered bay makes it suitable for sea bathing all year round.

Winter solstice: The day with the shortest number of daylight hours. In 1810 England, this fell on 22 December.

Discussion questions

1. Which character in the book did you like best? What was it that attracted you to them?

2. Peter and Meg fall in love with each other very soon after they meet. Do you believe in love at first sight? Why or why not?

3. Peter became friends with Jethro Hunt whilst studying together at school and the friendship lasted into adulthood. Are you still friends with people you went to school or college with? What do you think has made those friendships survive?

4. What Christmas traditions do you have in your family? Have these been passed down through the generations or have you created your own?

5. *If you spend your time trying to outdo others, you'll always be disappointed.* Would you agree with this statement? Why or why not?

6. Meg still trusted Peter, even after he'd told her he couldn't marry her. Why do you think she was able to do this?

7. *What a relief it was to stop pretending she was someone she wasn't. She hadn't realised how exhausting it had been.* In what circumstances are you tempted to wear a mask? Do you think it is always a bad thing? Would you agree it is exhausting to pretend to be someone you're not?

8. *Friends helped each other to do what was right.* Have you ever tried to help a friend to do what was right? How successful were you?

9. *He had to trust that God was still in control of his life, even if it didn't feel like it.* Does Peter's declaration of faith resonate with you? In what circumstances has your faith been tried? If you don't have a faith, how do you cope when life seems out of control?

10. *All kinds of mischief can result if people form assumptions and don't bother to find out if there's any truth in them.* How can we guard ourselves from making false assumptions about people?

About the author

Rachel Knowles loves happy endings. She first read Jane Austen's *Pride and Prejudice* at the age of thirteen and fell in love, not only with Mr Darcy, but with the entire Regency period.

She regularly gives talks on the Regency period, based on her extensive research, and is co-author of the popular Regency History blog.

Rachel lives in the beautiful Georgian seaside town of Weymouth, Dorset, on the south coast of England, with her husband, Andrew. They have four daughters and a growing number of grandchildren.

Sign up for Rachel's newsletter

Be the first to know about new releases, special offers and giveaways by signing up for Rachel's newsletter on RachelKnowlesauthor.com.

Follow Rachel on social media

amazon.com/author/rachelknowles

bookbub.com/authors/rachel-knowles

goodreads.com/rachelknowles

instagram.com/rachelknowlesauthor

facebook.com/rachelknowlesauthor

Also by Rachel Knowles

THE MERRY ROMANCES

https://mybook.to/TheMerryRomances

https://mybook.to/EMS

Historical Non-fiction

https://mybook.to/WRWDFU

Printed in Great Britain
by Amazon

35982325R00111